WOLF STORM

WOLF STORM

DEE GARRETSON

HARPER
An Imprint of HarperCollins Publishers

Library of Congress Cataloging-in-Publication Data is available.
ISBN 978-0-06-200032-3 (trade bdg.)

Typography by Larissa Lawrynenko
11 12 13 14 15 LP/RRDB 10 9 8 7 6 5 4 3 2 1

First Edition

For Dean

Acknowledgments

Thanks first to all my family, always a tremendous support, and a special thanks to my children, who help me see the world through different eyes. I am also fortunate to have some wonderful writer friends who have been there for critiquing, discussing ideas, and support when I needed it. So thanks to Jeanne Estridge, Lori Foster, Amanda Avutu, Bill MacFarland, Ann Abbott, and to all the writers at AW. You have all made this writing life much more fun. Thanks also to Shelli Caskey—I can't imagine ever writing a book that doesn't have animals in it, and it's great to know I can go to her for ideas and information. I would thank my cats too, for keeping me company, but since they just assume it's my job to give them all the attention they want, I won't bother.

Chapter 1

THE LAIR

CARPATHIAN MOUNTAINS, SLOVAKIA, EASTERN EUROPE

Snow lay thick in the ruins of the castle walls, drifting over the best hiding places. The creatures who lived there didn't know the broken stone was the work of men. The stench of humans had disappeared centuries ago. Occasional hikers who came to picnic in the summer never stayed long enough to embed their own scent. Those times the creatures faded into the shadows, waiting patiently, knowing the humans wouldn't linger. Now, in the depths of what seemed an endless winter, summer warmth was just a trace of a memory and food was so scarce, it was time to venture farther afield before starvation set in.

Chapter 2

PROWLING

ICE PLANET EARTH SET, SLOVAKIA

The wolf Boris pushed his nose into Stefan's hand, his breath warm against the coldness of Stefan's fingers. Stefan tried to keep his hand very still, just in case the animal mistook his fingers for a chew toy. The animals in the movie were supposed to be highly trained and perfectly safe, but still, a wolf was a wolf. "Um, good boy," he murmured. "Nice wolf." Boris licked his hand like he was testing its flavor potential. "Trust me," Stefan said. "You'd rather have wolf kibble."

Jeremy Cline, who played his younger brother, shifted around, bumping into Stefan. "Sorry, your sleeve is tickling my face," Jeremy said.

"Hold still," Raine Randolph hissed. Raine was supposed to be playing their demanding sister, and from what Stefan had seen, it wouldn't be a stretch for her. They were already behind in the filming schedule for the day because of Raine's fit about the placement of the metal barrette things in her hair. She'd made the hair person shift them around several times. Then she had complained about the boots she wore, because they didn't make her look tall enough. He knew famous stars were used to getting their way, but he hadn't expected a thirteen-year-old could get away with acting like she was queen of the world.

"The ramp is slippery! There isn't enough room," Jeremy said. The three of them, along with two wolves and the actor playing their grandfather, were crammed into the doorway of a mock space-ship, waiting for the director to tell them what to do. It wasn't even a whole spaceship, just one side of it, held up by wooden supports. Mark, the director, had explained it was too expensive to build a complete one for the exterior shots, but Stefan was still a little disappointed.

"I just want close-ups on the kids' faces," Mark said to one of the cameramen. "Capture their emotions when they see all the snow and the desolation." He turned toward them. "Okay, kids. Let's get in the mood here. You're the first humans to come back to a post-apocalyptic Earth in eons. You're devastated you were forced to leave your parents and your own planet behind, and you don't know how long you're going to be stuck on this frozen world. Earth is now in another ice age, and you don't know what you're facing. Up until the spaceship door opens, the reality of it hasn't hit you. All we want today is the looks on your faces when you realize just how bad the situation is.

"We'll put the ramp back up before the camera rolls. Then, when I call for action, the ramp comes down, and Stefan, you're out first with Boris. Raine and her wolf, Inky, go to your right, and Jeremy to your left. Jeremy, we'll get an establishing shot of you with your wolf later. There just isn't room on the ramp for all of them. The wolves will move to their marks, those bits of cloth fastened to the ramp, so follow their lead." He gestured to the other cameraman. "I want good coverage of the lead wolf early on. Boris is going to rock the screen when we do his fight shots. He is one mean-looking wolf when he snarls." As if

4

to disprove that, Boris licked Stefan's hand again and wagged his tail.

Stefan laughed and patted the wolf again, then acted like he was grabbing an invisible microphone. "You ain't nothing but a hound dog," he sang. Boris wagged his tail harder.

Jeremy giggled. "I recognize that one. It's the guy named Elvis who wore those sparkly white suits. My grandmother loves him." Raine didn't laugh. She hadn't laughed at Stefan's Elmo the Muppet imitation either, when they were having their costumes checked. She'd given him that "you're so immature" look girls perfected early on.

"Can you teach me how to do imitations?" Jeremy said, looking up at Stefan.

"Um, maybe," Stefan said. Jeremy was already showing too many signs of latching on to him, tagging after him and asking questions. The last thing Stefan wanted was some kid following him around all the time. He got enough of that at home from his little brothers. On his very first movie, he was going to take advantage of being on his own.

"Hold still, boys, please, so we can finish the light check," Mark said. "Stefan, remember, you're supposed to be the oldest. Without your father here, you're the leader of the group. The troops with you are loyal to your family and expect you to be in charge, so look confident." Stefan liked the idea of being in charge of his own troops, even if none of them were actually on set yet. It was easy enough to imagine a whole squadron of men behind him in the spaceship.

"Get the snow off the ramp before you take it up," Mark told one of the crew as he brushed the snow off his beard. The crew were all quickly turning to snowmen. The snow had been falling steadily, fine powdery flakes that coated people and surfaces within minutes. Stefan was glad he didn't have to be one of the people shoveling snow. That was usually his job back home, so it felt nice to watch someone else have to do it.

When the ramp was clear, Mark motioned for it to be taken it up. "Okay, let's try this."

Behind the raised ramp, Stefan closed his eyes, trying to envision being in a real spaceship. He heard Mark's muffled voice from the other side call, "Roll sound." Then silence. "Roll camera. Action!"

The ramp came down with a soft thump on the snow and Hans, the wolf trainer, signaled the animals to move. Stefan knew he wasn't supposed to look at the trainer, but the signal distracted him, and for a split second his eyes shifted to the man.

"Cut!" Mark said. "Raine, that was perfect. Stefan, maybe a little less dismayed, please, and don't look at Hans. You are afraid, but you don't want anyone to know. Put your hand on Boris's neck; the wolves are the symbol of your family's power and he's also your best friend. Hold on just a minute. I want the camera shifted a bit."

Stefan tried to think of how someone would look acting brave and confident. His mind went blank. He stared up into the mountains surrounding the set. At least it didn't take too much acting for the dismay part. The set was in the middle of nowhere, a nowhere buried in several feet of snow. When he'd finally gotten the word he had been cast, and that they were going to start filming on location in the country of Slovakia, in Eastern Europe, he'd had to look it up on a map. The set was at an old ski resort in the Carpathian Mountains that had been closed for years. The whole place was stark and forbidding, a flat plateau halfway up a mountain, surrounded by other mountains and accessible only by a narrow switchback road cut through a cliff.

The muscles on Boris's neck tensed underneath

his hand and the wolf strained toward the snack truck. Stefan was puzzled. The array of food was incredible, bagels and chocolate and yogurt and granola bars and fruit, but he didn't think there was anything there a wolf would want, no platters of deer burgers or sheep steaks.

"Let's try again," Mark said. "Once the ramp is up, get the snow off their hair and faces so it looks like they have just arrived."

This time when the ramp came down, Stefan moved forward and glimpsed something peering around the side of the snack truck. It looked like one of the wolves but was too shaggy, and it was gray. All the set wolves were black, or at least all the ones he had seen. Had one of the spare ones gotten loose?

"Cut. Stefan, don't look like you see something," Mark said. "Remember, there's nothing but snow and ice."

Boris growled, his attention focused in the direction of the food truck, and Stefan could tell he had seen the animal too. The animal ducked behind the truck and Boris crouched down like he was getting ready to take off after it.

Chapter 3

BREAK A LEG

Stefan grabbed the wolf's collar just as Hans came up and ordered the wolf to sit. Boris obeyed.

"What's wrong with him?" Mark asked Hans.

"I think there's a wolf out there, a wild one," Stefan said. "Behind the snack truck." Everyone turned to look, but Stefan couldn't see the creature any longer.

"I saw something as well." Cecil Braithwaite, the actor playing the grandfather, moved forward and pointed. "It slunk off into that stand of spruce trees near the base of the ski slope."

"No, that's impossible." The trainer frowned. "Wolves wouldn't get this close to people. They do everything they can to avoid contact, even when people are on their territory. Probably just a dog, maybe even a feral one. If it is, that's not good. The pack doesn't like strange dogs."

"If that was a dog, it was doing a marvelous job imitating a wolf," Cecil said. "Large, furry, rather wolfish expression. Exactly the look to be cast in a Little Red Riding Hood production."

"The majority of the wolves in the Carpathians are much farther east." The trainer paced back and forth, looking at the cliffs in the distance. "If a wolf pack has moved into this area, my wolves aren't going to be happy. They can smell them from an incredible distance."

"Maybe there are wolves around here," Mark said. "We didn't check on that. I thought wolves were rare everywhere now, since they've practically been hunted to extinction in the States. I just assumed the name of the place referred to the way it was centuries ago."

"What *is* the name?" Cecil asked.

"It's called *Vlk Vrch* in Slovak; it means 'Wolf Mountain,'" Mark said. "That's where I got the idea to put the wolves in the script, when we found this location."

Everyone just looked at each other. Finally, Mark said, "Any of the local crew know about wolves around here?" Suddenly everyone was speaking in English and some languages Stefan didn't recognize.

"This man knows." A cameraman stepped forward, motioning to another crew member.

"He says of course there are wolves. The mountains are full of them, but he says not to worry. They aren't seen very frequently."

Another man in the back of the group spoke up, his English heavily accented. "My father said he heard from a friend that the villagers claim they heard a child in another village was carried off by a wolf."

"Oh, that's ridiculous," Hans said, scowling. "Wolves don't attack people, except in fairy tales. Even if there was a wolf out there, it won't come back. I'm telling you, there are very few reasons a wolf would purposely seek out people. They hate strange wolves in their territory, but they still won't come near us. They'll do anything possible to avoid humans."

Even though Stefan had only caught a glimpse of the animal, it hadn't looked like it was trying to avoid people. It had been watching them, and he didn't think it had accidentally found itself on a movie set.

"What do you recommend, Hans?" Mark asked. "We don't want our wolves distracted."

"Let's wait and see how my group performs," the trainer said. "We've never been in this situation before. I just can't give you a prediction."

"Okay, we'll keep going." Mark switched back to director mode. "Let's try again. Stefan, while you're walking down the ramp, gaze out into the distance. Narrow your eyes a bit, like you're analyzing the landscape."

The ramp was too slippery, made of some sort of coppery metal, and their boots had no treads on them. On the next take Stefan almost lost his balance and ended up waving his arms around.

"Cut! Let's try again."

They tried eleven more takes, and Stefan could tell none of them were making Mark happy. It was hard for him to pretend he was on a desolate, dangerous planet when fifty people were standing in front of him, sipping coffee and checking their text messages. His aunt, Heather, on set with him as his guardian, was busy as usual flirting, this time with some guy in a leather jacket and a multicolored stocking hat. Heather's latest hair color, light pink, was especially distracting, because every time she moved it was like watching a puff of cotton candy bobbing around.

"Cut! Stefan, remember when you did that imitation for me when you first auditioned?" Mark said. "The one of Gregory Peck that I liked?"

Stefan felt his face growing hot. He had been so nervous the first time he met Mark, he did a whole riff of goofy imitations of old-time movie actors, everyone from Jerry Lewis to John Wayne. It was something he did at home to make his mom laugh on those particularly grim days when the younger kids and the bills got too much for her. Mark went crazy over the imitations because it turned out he was an old movie buff, which, when Stefan thought about it afterward, was not really surprising for a director. Stefan hadn't expected him to bring it up in front of everyone though.

"I remember," Stefan mumbled.

"Terrific! That's what we need. Young Gregory Peck in *The Keys of the Kingdom*. Resolute, determined."

They took their places again. While they were waiting for Mark to yell "Action," Stefan heard a faint squeaky sound coming from Jeremy.

"Are you whistling?" Raine hissed. "Be quiet."

"I can't," Jeremy whispered. "The cold is

making my asthma act up. I think I'm allergic to the wolves, too. There weren't wolves in the script when I auditioned."

"We can stop if you need some medicine," Cecil said. "Actors must take care of themselves. You are the tool of your trade."

Jeremy coughed and then said, "There, I'm better. Besides, my dad will get mad if I make them stop. He says I'll get a name for being unprofessional." Stefan had already pegged Jeremy's dad as the intense kind. Even though the man was always glued to his cell phone, he watched everyone like a coach deciding who was going to make the team and who was going to be cut.

"How old are you? Eight? Nine?" Stefan asked. "You're just a kid; you don't need to be professional all the time. I don't think it would be that big a deal to ask to stop because you can't breathe." Stefan didn't want to see a major asthma attack. One of his friends at home carried around an EpiPen for his asthma, and Stefan always hoped it wouldn't be needed when they were together. He knew it was wimpy of him, but the thought of watching someone jab himself with a needle pen made his stomach turn. He'd never be a doctor.

"Everything okay, kids?" Their teacher on set, Amanda Rissert, came up to them. She tutored them for three hours a day, and she was also supposed to be what she called their "advocate," making sure everyone followed the strict rules about what kids could and couldn't do safely on movie sets.

"Jeremy?" Stefan said. He wasn't going to rat the kid out about the asthma if it wasn't a big deal, but he wanted Jeremy to speak up if he needed medicine.

"We're good." Jeremy gave a thumbs-up.

"Are you cold?" Amanda asked. "The temperature has dropped quite a bit since you started."

"Yes, I'm cold," Raine grumbled. "It's freezing here, and I'm wearing a weird furry garbage bag decorated with bottle caps."

Stefan hadn't thought of the costumes that way, but Raine wasn't too far off. The long overcoats they wore were kind of fun to stride around in, except the fabric *was* weird. It was futuristic looking, both shiny and soft at the same time, and each outfit was covered with small metal disks etched with an outline of a wolf's head. He knew the disks were related to some special effect, but they hadn't seen that yet.

"Aren't you wearing long underwear?" Amanda said.

"I am, but it's not working," Raine said. "I hate the cold."

"Do you want a break to warm up?"

"No, let's just get this done." Raine looked at Stefan. "Let's hope it doesn't take that much longer to get it right."

"It won't," Stefan said. "I've got it now."

When Mark yelled "Action" again, Stefan knew he could do it. The ramp came down and he stepped forward with Boris, doing his best Gregory Peck imitation. A high-pitched bark came from the crowd, and both Boris and Inky, the other wolf, growled.

"Cut!" Mark yelled. "Now what!"

"Sorry, Mark," Raine's mother said from the background. "I thought Mr. Snuggums needed some fresh air." She held up Raine's dog, which was some sort of miniature squashed-face breed. "He almost never barks, do you, sweetie? Those big bad old wolves won't hurt you." Mrs. Randolph's nasally voice switched to crooning baby talk.

"Mother!" Raine said, as if she was embarrassed. Stefan would have been in her place. At least his own mother never did things like that. He couldn't imagine his mom talking baby talk to real babies, much less dogs.

Raine's dog barked again, struggling to get free, and Inky, Raine's wolf, whined. The wolf trainer looked furious. "Mrs. Randolph, it would be a good idea if you kept that dog away from the wolves. Wolves don't like animals that aren't part of their own pack. It upsets them to see a dog they don't know."

"They'll just have to get used to him." Mrs. Randolph made kissing noises at the dog. "Raine needs Mr. Snuggums on set with her. It's in her contract."

"Mom, I do not need him," Raine said, a clear edge of anger in her voice. "Why don't you take him inside? It's too cold out here."

Stefan wasn't sure the wolves would think of Raine's pet as an actual dog. He doubted if they'd ever seen any animal dressed in a beret, knitted boots, and a cheetah-print dog sweater that matched the coat Raine's mother wore. It didn't smell like a dog either. Even from ten feet away, some sickly sweet odor emanated from it, as if it had been dipped in perfume.

"Please, Mrs. Randolph," the assistant director

said. "We'd really like to break for lunch soon, and we need to get this shot if we are going to keep on schedule and make the day."

The producer, a man named Sherman Gregson, who seemed to wear a permanent frown, put his arm around Raine's mother. "You're looking cold too. Why don't you go on inside?"

Jeremy coughed again, so hard that he lost his balance, bumping into Stefan. Stefan put a hand out to catch him, but the slight shift in his own weight made one foot slip out from under him. Trying to stabilize himself, he fell the other way, into Inky and Raine. It was like a domino effect; they all went down off the side of ramp into the snow. As he felt himself falling, Stefan instinctively reached out to catch something to break the fall and grabbed hold of one of the lights. It came down after him and landed with sickening thud, right on Inky, just as the wolf was scrambling out from under Raine. The wolf struggled to get up, then dropped to the ground.

Chapter 4

WARNINGS

Immediately, the trainer and his assistant were down in the snow beside the wolf. Everyone else froze in place.

"I'm sorry," Stefan said, scrambling to his feet.

"Get out of my way!" the trainer shouted.

Stefan backed up. "I just grabbed on to the light without thinking. I didn't think it would fall over. I didn't mean to hurt him." He couldn't tell at first if Inky was breathing, and then he saw the wolf's chest rising and falling.

He was about to explain how Jeremy had bumped into him, but then he noticed the kid's face, scrunched up like he was about to cry. Jeremy's dad was gripping his shoulder.

"Is he . . . is he dead?" Jeremy asked.

"I'm sorry," Stefan said again. "I slipped."

No one answered. Boris leaped off the ramp and positioned himself near Inky.

"I can't tell if any of his ribs are broken," Hans said. "I'll have to take him to a vet with an X-ray machine. Somebody find me the closest one. We'll need some sort of stretcher."

There was a burst of activity; then Stefan heard a babble of voices as everyone around him pulled out their cell phones. Within a few minutes some of the crew brought over a piece of plywood covered with a blanket, and the trainer and his assistant eased the wolf onto it. Inky whimpered but didn't move. As they lifted up the board and moved off, Boris barked. Inky didn't respond.

As the wolf was loaded into the back of a van, there was more discussion and hand waving, and then two crew members climbed into the back. The snow had left a few inches on the ground since the last time the parking lot had been plowed, and the van's back wheels skidded.

"I hope the road down the mountain isn't too bad," Mark said. "We're not exactly on a main highway." Mark was right about that, Stefan thought. When they had driven up to the lodge, crossing an old bridge right out of the village at the base of the mountain, the road had narrowed almost to a single lane. Once it passed a cluster of cottages and one small farm, it had also been bumpy and broken up in places, like no one had used it since the ski resort closed.

The assistant trainer came over to Mark. "I need to put Boris back in his cage now," he said. "Hans doesn't want me working with the wolves until he gets back."

"Of course," Mark said. The assistant fastened a collar around Boris and then led him off. Stefan didn't know what he should say.

"You know, Mark, that ramp is impossibly slippery," Cecil said. "The only reason I didn't fall is because I was in the back on the level part. Can we add something either to the ramp or the soles of the boots to help? I don't fancy a broken bone at my age."

"You're right, Cecil. We didn't think that through enough, and it will be fixed by tomorrow. It's all right, everyone. I'm sure the wolf will be okay. It's not your fault, Stefan. Okay?"

"Right," Stefan mumbled.

"Change of plans," Mark said. "Too much snow anyway for now. We'll pick up that scene tomorrow, but after lunch we're going to try a little rehearsal of the scene where the frost demons attack. We'll just need Raine and Stefan. Good job, Jeremy. Let's call lunch." That triggered a mad rush to the door of the main lodge, an old building that everyone said looked exactly like a Swiss chalet. Stefan had never seen a chalet, but he figured they meant all the fancy woodwork around the roof and the rickety balconies off the upper stories.

"Let's get you all inside and get you warm," Amanda said.

"I may never be warm again." Raine gave an exaggerated shiver. "Amanda, I don't know what happened to my copy of the book of Slovak folktales. I want to do my paper on them. Can you get me another copy?" They walked away, busy talking.

Stefan hung back, not interested in eating. Nothing like accidentally taking out a wolf to kill a person's appetite. All he wanted to do was find a place where he could be out of sight. Inside the lodge, everyone was heading to the dining room, so Stefan went the other way. The lodge was a massive old stone and wooden building unlike any hotel Stefan had ever seen, all dark, carved woodwork and stone floors. The main area, a big open space in what used to be the lobby, still had a reception desk and a wall of wooden mail slots behind it. Off to one side was a giant fireplace with sofas and chairs scattered around it. At the end of the room, near where it opened into what was now an empty office, was a bowed window like something out of a castle, except it looked out the back of the lodge to the parking lot behind the building.

Stefan pulled one of the big chairs to the window, turning it away from anyone's view. There was nothing much to see but cars, movie trailers, and motor homes, all lined up on one side of the parking lot, and one big evergreen tree on the other side of a stone wall at the back of the lot. He guessed the wall was supposed to warn people there was a sharp drop-off right beyond it. The lot was built almost right to the edge of the cliff separating their part of the mountain from the lower slope.

"There you are," Heather said. "Tough luck about the wolf."

So much for hiding out. "I know." He didn't want to get into a discussion about Inky.

"You did great though, standing there and all. I can't believe how many times they made you do it. I thought it was just fine the first time." Stefan didn't answer, hoping Heather would get the hint to go away. Her phone rang. "Hey, Sis. He's right here." She listened for a moment and then said, "It's your mom."

"Is something wrong?" He and his mom had arranged beforehand that they would try to keep the cell phone charges down. Calling Slovakia from Massachusetts wasn't cheap.

"He's got his costume on." Heather gestured at Stefan as if his mom could see him over the phone. "That's probably why he doesn't have his phone. You should see him; you wouldn't even recognize your little boy." Stefan was glad no one was close enough to overhear his aunt. At fourteen he was hardly a little boy. "He looks so much taller and older." Heather held her hand up over her head like she was trying to show his mom how tall he was. "Okay, I'll let you talk to him. Here he is."

"Mom?"

"Hi, sweetie, how's it going?"

He could hear the sound of the television and his brother Jake yelling "Watch out!" in the background. Jake was only four and still thought the actors on screen needed help during times of danger.

"I'm fine, Mom," Stefan said. He wasn't going to tell her about the wolf. "How's everyone there?" He heard Jake scream, "Run! The dogcatcher is right behind you!"

"Jake, please, not so loud!" his mom shouted. "Stefan, I'm sorry to bother you, but there's something wrong with the water pressure in the house. I'm going to call the plumber in the morning. Since you talked to him last time, I wanted to know if there was anything special I should tell him."

Stefan wasn't surprised to hear something else at the house was broken, but he wished it hadn't happened now. He and his mom between them tried to figure out how to keep the place from falling apart, even though neither one of them really knew what they were doing. "No, don't call the plumber. Call Neil Hadley instead. It's probably a bad pressure controller like last time, and Neil will fix it a lot cheaper than the plumber." Stefan couldn't wait for his next paycheck to come through. Even though his mom had said they weren't spending any of his money on the house, he was going to make sure they did at least get a new pump for the well and a new roof.

"Okay," his mom said, "if you're sure Neil can fix

it." A blast of noise drowned her out. "Jake, turn down the television! Stefan, I saw Aaron with his mother at the grocery store. He can't wait to hear all about what you're doing. You should email him when you get a chance."

"Sure." He doubted Aaron actually wanted to hear from him. It was Aaron who wanted to be the actor and who had convinced Stefan to go with him to the big open casting call in Boston for the movie. Stefan had just gone along to see what it was like, so he had been floored when someone at the tryouts pulled him out of the line and interviewed him, giving him lines to read. Stefan didn't think Aaron would ever forgive him for getting the part.

"I have to go, sweetie. Are you sure you are okay? Your voice sounds funny."

"It's just the connection, Mom. I'm fine. Talk to you soon." He handed the phone back to Heather.

"We should eat," she said.

"You go ahead. I'm not very hungry."

"Are you sure? Are you sick? You're always hungry."

"I'll eat later. There's food everywhere here." He could always get something from the snack truck. It was parked outside the front of the lodge, close to the base of the main ski slope, and now that everyone was inside eating, there wouldn't be too many people out there to face.

After Heather left, Stefan sank into the chair, hoping no one else would find him. The snow was still coming down, lighter now, but still the sort of steady snow that back home would have led to days off from school. There wasn't much activity out by the trailers in the parking lot, except for a crew person loading a camera into one. He'd been surprised at the amount of stuff needed to make a movie. There were at least ten big trailers and motor homes full of equipment and props.

A semitruck pulled up, sliding to a stop on the far side of the lot, away from all the other trailers and motor homes. The props crew opened up the back and lowered a ramp. Stefan moved closer to the window and rubbed it to get a better look.

Two men wheeled out a small trailer, the kind people pulled behind their cars when they were hauling boats. On it was something like an over-sized snowmobile without any runners, with a clear plastic canopy over the driver's seat. It had to be one of the snow skimmer props, the little vehicles that they'd pretend to fly around to explore the surface of the planet. Even if the skimmers couldn't really hover over the surface of the snow, it would be fantastic to act like he was flying one. That sort of thing he just knew he wouldn't mess up.

The men covered the skimmer up with a tarp before Stefan could get a good look. When they had situated the trailer in a cleared spot, they wheeled another one down, covering it up as well.

"Hi!" Jeremy said. Stefan hadn't heard the kid come up. He was going to have to find a better place to keep away from people. "What are you doing?"

"Sitting, you know, looking out the window."

"Oh. Can I look too?"

"There's not much to see but snow." If he told Jeremy about the snow skimmers, he wouldn't be able to get rid of him. A gust of wind shook the window and a mound of snow slid off the roof, covering up some piece of equipment in a crate.

"I wish it snowed where we live in California. Isn't it great?" Jeremy said.

"Pretty great. I'm really glad I'm not the one who has to shovel it though. Shouldn't you be eating lunch?" Stefan asked.

"I already did. There's too much weird food in there, so I just had a bagel. Besides, my dad is in

28

a really crabby mood. He's yelling at whoever he's talking to on the phone."

"You know what? I'll let you have my seat." Stefan got up. "I'm going to go check on the wolves."

"Can I come with you? I want to talk to Brad again too. He didn't finish telling me about how they train the wolves."

"Who's Brad?"

"He's the assistant trainer." Jeremy looked at Stefan like he was already supposed to know that, but Stefan didn't remember ever hearing the man's name. There were way too many people working on the movie for him to remember names yet.

As soon as they got outside, Stefan wished he had bothered to put on his coat. The wind was biting into his face. They made their way over to the wolves' motor home, Jeremy talking the whole time. "Guess why they parked their motor home at the front of the building away from the parking lot."

Stefan hadn't thought about it. "I don't know," he said.

"One of the wolves doesn't like the sound of trucks, so they couldn't park it in the parking lot. There's too many vehicles coming and going.

They like to be by themselves."

"Oh," Stefan said.

"Do you think you have to go to college to be a wolf trainer?" Jeremy asked.

"I don't know."

"Don't you think that would be a great job? What are you going to be when you grow up?"

"I don't know. Probably an engineer or something. Look, I'm getting cold. Let's hurry." He hoped if they speeded up the kid would quit talking.

"Tomorrow there might be a bad storm," Jeremy said. "I heard the producer, Sherman, say most of it is going to miss us, but it's still going to snow tons. Do you think they will let us get some sleds and go sledding?"

"Maybe." Stefan felt a momentary pang of homesickness. This much snow would have brought everyone out to the hill by the school, to pile on sleds and snowboards, racing until it got too dark to see. The old wooden bobsleds their grandfather had fixed up for them weren't the showiest, but they were fast. And he had attempted snowboarding over the past year, even though the hill wasn't long enough to be like a real slope.

Now that he thought about it, the ski slope in

front of the lodge would make a terrific sledding slope, if you weren't afraid of a little speed, actually a lot of speed. It was so steep it must have been one of those runs for expert skiers. It would be fun to try it out with sleds.

"It might even be a blizzard," Jeremy said.

"Are you sure they said a blizzard?" Stefan had experienced one blizzard back home and didn't want to be near another. He'd only been about seven at the time and had been scared their house was either going to be blown away by the wind or collapse under the weight of the snow.

"That's what I heard. Sherman doesn't want the filming to stop because he says it costs too much money, so he wants somebody to go get more snow shovels and rent some snow blowers. He's sending people off to get all sorts of other supplies too so we can keep working."

"Great. Snowblowers in a blizzard. That's not going to do much good." Stefan knew it was the producer's job to keep the movie on budget, but if the man thought they'd be able to accomplish anything in a blizzard, he was in for a big surprise.

Chapter 5

STRANGERS

The gray wolf lingered among the trees, watching. The hunger gnawed at him, and the pain, but there were too many humans, and humans were dangerous. The agony in his skull never stopped now. He had killed the invader who attacked him, a lone wolf trying to take over the pack, but the pain remained, lancing through his head into his eye. Foreign shadows sometimes jumped across the eye, enraging him, and he snapped at them, trying to protect himself against those who would bring him down, but he never caught them. Now there was a new threat. These strange wolves smelled of humans, and they had no place in his land. He had to protect the pack's territory before the cubs arrived in the spring. He knew he needed to feed to regain his strength, and then he would overcome them.

Chapter 6

MISTAKES

Jeremy stopped Stefan right before they reached the door of the motor home. "I'm sorry I bumped into you and made Inky get hurt. I wanted to tell Mark it was all my fault, but my dad said I didn't need to."

"It's okay." Stefan knocked on the door. "It was just an accident." Music was blasting inside, so he knocked again, harder.

Brad opened the door, heat rushing out around him. Wearing a Hawaiian print shirt over a sweater and sunglasses propped on top of his head, he looked more like a misplaced surfer than a wolf trainer. "Hey, what's up?" he asked.

"Hi," Stefan said, feeling awkward. "I was just

wondering if you've heard from Hans. You know, if he's called from the vet yet."

"It's way too soon. The nearest vet with an X-ray is ninety miles away. With all this crazy snow, it will take him a while to get there," Brad said, strumming an invisible guitar.

"We feel bad," Jeremy said.

"Don't blame yourself. We know it was an accident. Hans got all worked up because these wolves are like his kids. He overreacts, but he'll calm down when he thinks about it."

"Can we come in and see the wolves?" Jeremy asked.

Brad waved them in and then flopped in one of the chairs, humming away, like he'd forgotten they were there. Stefan hadn't expected the motor home to be so deluxe. The front part of it had a kitchen, a table, and a seating area, like a living room. Each wolf had its own large cage, and they were all lying down, curled up in huge plaid dog beds. Boris stood up and wagged his tail when Stefan went over to him. At least the wolf didn't hold Inky's injury against him.

"Don't the wolves mind that Inky isn't here?" Jeremy asked.

"They're used to not being together all the time,

and Inky's a bit of a troublemaker anyway, at least to Natasha." Brad pointed to a wolf that had one white patch on its chest. "Natasha is the alpha female, and she makes it her job to keep everyone else in line. Inky likes to challenge her, and that really bugs her."

"Do you think it will be a problem if there are wild wolves around?" Stefan reached his hand through the cage to scratch Boris's neck. Natasha growled at him, staring at his hand like she wanted to bite it. Boris didn't mind though, so Stefan kept scratching, keeping his eyes away from the other wolf. He knew enough about aggressive dogs to know you didn't stare them in the face, because they thought it was a challenge.

"Nah, they're not going to care about other wolves. Our wolves have been raised in captivity since they were pups. They'll just think other wolves are like dogs, and they may act a little territorial, but it will be fine. Now that they're inside, away from that stray dog, or wolf, they calmed down, especially Boris."

"Boris seemed more nervous about the wolf than Inky," Jeremy said.

"He's what we call the alpha male of the pack, because he's the oldest. If he thinks the pack is in danger, he gets very disturbed, and the rest of them follow his lead. But when he calms down, they do too. Tomorrow I'll lead him around the set so he can be sure there aren't any outsiders here. That will satisfy him. Stefan, that girl with you, is she your sister?"

The change of subject confused Stefan. The only girl on the set was Raine, and even though she and Stefan looked alike, both with hair and eyes so dark they matched the wolves, Brad had to know who she was. Her face was on the cover of magazines all the time.

"You mean Raine?" he asked.

"Not Raine! She's a kid! The cute girl with the pink hair."

Heather. He hadn't thought of her as a girl. She was at least twenty-five. "She's my aunt."

"Oh." It sounded like Brad was going to say something else, but Jeremy interrupted.

"Who's this one?" Jeremy went over to a cage where the smallest wolf lay, another black one, with a brownish cast to the ends of its fur. "She looks sad."

Stefan didn't think the wolf looked particularly sad, maybe just steamed from the heat. He could bet wolves in the wild didn't like saunas.

"That's Phoebe. She's been moping around lately, but we don't know why. She's the omega wolf, sort of the lowest on the totem pole, you might say. No, that's not right. I'm really the omega wolf, come to think of it, at least according to Hans. Hans wouldn't rank me above her."

"Who decides which wolf gets what place?" Jeremy knelt down by Phoebe. The wolf looked up but didn't move.

"If they were really wild wolves, the ranking would sort itself out on which ones were the oldest, and the strongest. A lot of times the alpha female is the best hunter, and she's often the most aggressive, even more than the alpha male. It's amazing to watch wolves hunt." Brad sat forward and his face lit up. "Their teamwork is phenomenal, choreographed even. First, they follow a herd, deciding which animal is the weakest. Then they go after that one, and they take turns wearing down the prey, until they can all move in for the kill."

"That's awful!" Jeremy's voice was full of disgust.

"Sorry, dude, that's what wolves do. They're carnivores and hunters, and it's the way nature works. It ain't all fluffy bunnies and rainbows.

Besides, wolves keep the population of other animals under control, animals like elk. Stefan, your aunt, you know . . ." Brad's voice trailed off as he got up, took off his sunglasses, and smoothed back his hair, glancing at a mirror over the table.

"Yeah, I know her," Stefan said, amused.

"Does she have a boyfriend or is she married? You know, is she attached?"

The guy in the leather coat Heather had been flirting with probably wasn't an attachment yet. "No, why?" He really didn't need to ask. His mom always said Heather collected boyfriends like some women collected shoes.

"Just wondering." Brad punched Stefan on the arm and grinned.

"Stefan, why is your aunt with you, and not your mom or dad?" Jeremy asked.

"My mom couldn't leave her job, she's a nurse, and my dad . . . travels a lot for work, business, you know." He wasn't going to tell them the truth. He had never figured out the right way to say, "My dad took off, and I don't know and don't care where he is." It was the sort of thing that made a conversation drag.

"Hey, if you're done visiting with our gang, let's get out of here. I'm hungry." They followed Brad outside. Stefan ducked just in time as a snow-ball whizzed by his head. Two of the crew were running around out front of the lodge, laughing crazily, pelting each other with snowballs, like they had discovered some rare game.

"There you are!" Amanda rushed up to them, as if they'd been lost. "It's time for Stefan to get back to work, and Jeremy, your father is looking for you."

"Work, right," Stefan said. Rehearsing in front of Mark and who knows how many other people was not going to be easy. He hadn't realized act-ing involved so much more than just doing weird accents and imitating facial expressions.

Amanda must have sensed some of his reluc-tance. "It's just a rehearsal. Mark wants you to work with the weapons master. That should be exciting!" Her voice had the fake perkiness of a teacher saying a test was easy, right before you got shot down by an essay question on the Renais-sance.

"I guess," he said, thinking of all the ways he could embarrass himself in front of an expert.

"It will! Mark says you've been training at home, so you should enjoy getting to use your new skills." He had to admit he had been looking forward to the fight scenes. Before the filming started, the production company had arranged for him to take the train into Boston on Saturdays to an aikido studio for lessons. One of the weapons he would use in the movie was similar to an ancient Japanese weapon called a *tanto*, which was like a combination of a knife and a short sword. After a month of practice, he wasn't as proficient at the moves as he wanted to be, but it had been fun to work on them.

Raine was already out in front of the spaceship, talking to Mark and Sherman. She didn't say anything to him.

"Stefan, I didn't see you at lunch," Mark said. "Everything okay?"

"Fine." His stomach chose that moment to let out a huge growl, loud enough for everyone to hear, and he realized he should have eaten something. It might be a long time until a break.

"You're not getting sick, are you?" Sherman asked. "We're getting behind schedule."

"No, I'm fine." Stefan always had the feeling Sherman wasn't too crazy about him being cast in the movie. The producer rarely spoke directly to Stefan and when he did, it was never just friendly conversation.

41

"Good," Mark said, "I was just telling Raine we should all have dinner together tonight, Cecil and Jeremy too, so you all can get to know each other better. I know it's hard to act as if you are related to someone when you don't even know them. On the last movie I directed, the kids had such a fantastic time together, they felt like a real family by the end."

Stefan didn't know how to answer. He just couldn't imagine considering any of them like his family. Raine didn't say anything either. Her face expressed exactly how little she thought of the whole "let's be a family" idea.

"Good!" Mark acted as if they had agreed. "Tomorrow we'll film in an area that hasn't been trampled down, but I wanted you to rehearse first where it won't be so difficult to get around in the snow." A lean man in a dark ski jacket walked up. "Here's what we need," Mark said. "Stefan, Raine, this is Randy, the fight coordinator. You're going to like this scene, Stefan. Randy, show these two what they are working with."

Randy opened a case and drew out something that looked like an intricately carved leather sword hilt.

"Where's the blade?" Stefan asked.

"That's the best part." Randy grasped the hilt and shifted his fingers slightly. A gleaming silver blade extended from the handle in one smooth motion, like a telescope extending. There were etched wolf heads on the blade, just like on the costumes. Stefan was amazed at the amount of work that had gone into it. Mark was famous for his attention to detail in every aspect of the movies he directed.

"Isn't that fantastic?" Mark said. "See the indents in the blade? That's where we will put in the effects of a laser-type bullet during the editing. It's an all-purpose weapon."

"We took the idea from the tanto you've been training with, Stefan, and adapted it to make it more sci-fi appropriate." Randy waved the sword in a complicated pattern so fast that the image of it blurred. "These were designed to be what a weapon might look like in the future. The problem with traditional weapons is that you have to keep a grip on them, and if you drop them in a real fight, you're dead. That's why these are going to be attached to your wrists by arm guards that are a modern take on an archer's buckler. Here, let me get one on you."

Stefan held out his arm, and Randy fastened

the guard on, talking the whole time. "We'll add the glimmer to the blade during postproduction by computer, so it will look more futuristic. The hilt fastens in here." The fight coordinator clicked it into place for Stefan. "These aren't sharp, but keep them away from each other's faces. You know, the old 'they could take someone's eye out' problem."

Stefan turned his arm back and forth, trying to get a feel for the right motions.

"Since this scene involves a surprise attack," Mark said, "you won't be using any of the shields we have. Those will be for later." Stefan tried to concentrate on Mark's words, but he was so entranced with the sword it was hard to focus. "Here's what you will be fighting."

A crew member reached into a container. He lifted out a thing about the size of an eagle. It looked like a cross between a pterodactyl and a giant bat, except it was a shimmery silver color, and it had a long beak with fangs. Its eyes were the creepiest part of it; they were an iridescent sickly yellow and shaped like snake eyes.

"Love these," Mark said. "They don't have a real scientific-type name in the script, because when your people land on the planet, you don't know what they are called. One of the soldiers names them 'frost devils' after he gets attacked by them."

Stefan thought they looked more like they should be named "batosaurs." They were great. He could just imagine his little brothers pretending to fly small action figure versions of them.

Mark waved the batosaur around like he was flying it. "This will take a bit of practice; that's why we have several of these. We'll be controlling the wings and the mouth remotely to keep them flapping. If you press the hidden trigger right here"—he pointed at the creature's left eye—"a lovely mess of alien innards will burst out so it will look like you killed it. Okay, here's the sequence. Stefan, you're caught outside and running back toward the spaceship when one of these dive-bombs you. You'll grab hold of the creature by the neck and wrestle with it. Twist and turn as if it's attacking you. We'll add in some of the effects later, but your movements need to convince us the thing is alive. Pretend the frost devil is very powerful and it forces you to your knees." Mark knelt down on the ground to demonstrate.

"Raine, you're going to be dancing around trying to get at it, but you can't because you don't want to injure your brother." Stefan couldn't help but glance at Raine. He didn't know if she had a real brother or not, but he was guessing she wouldn't be the kind to worry too much about injuring one.

"Then, Raine," Mark continued, "you'll pull out your weapon but you won't be able to use it because you can't get a clear shot. Stefan, maneuver so you can extend your weapon and stab the creature in the side. This one has a retractable blade so it will look like it's piercing the skin." He pushed on the tip and it slid right back into the hilt. "Got that?" Stefan wasn't sure he had but he nodded his head anyway.

"Now, this is the good part." Mark was so excited he looked like he wanted to do the scene himself. "Once you think the frost devil is dead, you drop it, but right before you do, push the eye, so that as it falls to the ground, the guts will spew out of it. Let's try it!"

At first Stefan felt ridiculous struggling with a plastic alien batosaur, but then he slipped into the feeling. If he concentrated on the sinister eyes, he could really believe it was dangerous.

"Good!" Mark yelled. "Now fall down to your knees and get your weapon out, but don't make it look too easy."

Stefan managed to do the right hand motion to click the sword into place, and then he stabbed it at the creature, using his other hand to click the button on the eye. But the neon green guts that spewed out of it startled him so much, he pushed the creature away from him, right into Raine. Alien goo shot out, covering her nose and her mouth, dripping down onto her costume.

"I'm sorry, Raine!" Stefan said. "I'm really sorry! Wow, they do look like intestines. Gross."

She stood there, wiping her face, and then, with a voice full of cold fury, said, "That's it. I've had it. I'm not working with amateurs. Stefan goes or I do."

Chapter 7

CREATIONS

Raine stomped away, pieces of intestine dripping into the snow, staining it green. Immediately a score of people surrounded her, their voices raised.

"Raine, wait!" Sherman hurried after her, giving Stefan a disgusted look as he passed by.

"I'm sorry," Stefan said. "It just surprised me." He tried to keep his voice even, like it was no big deal.

"It's okay." Mark sounded tired. "We should have shown you the effect first."

The location manager came up to them. "Mark, we're having some trouble with one of the permits to film. Can you and Sherman come into town? We need you both to spread some charm and make nice with the mayor."

"Okay, but what's the latest on the weather?"

"Depends on which way the wind shifts."

"Maybe we'll get lucky. Stefan, when I get back for dinner, we'll talk."

Stefan just nodded his head and waited to head back to the lodge until everyone else had gone away from the rehearsal area. He sighed, knowing he had to go apologize, even if it had been an accident.

Inside the lodge the costume people were hovering around Raine, dabbing at her with towels. Her mother gave directions, which everyone ignored. Raine wasn't even noticing them, brushing at them like they were flies.

"Raine, sweetheart, it's just the first day. Give him a chance," Sherman said.

"That's it. I've had it. He's not going to work out. Get rid of him." Raine put her hands on her hips. "I'm not going to work with an amateur."

"Let's just all calm down here." Sherman's voice sounded wary, like he was worried Raine was going to have a tantrum.

Stefan walked up to her and tried to get her attention. "Raine, I'm really sorry. It just surprised me. You aren't hurt, right?"

She ignored him. "I will not calm down! If the movie tanks because of him, we're all in trouble. We all know he wasn't hired because he could act; he was only hired because he looks like me! Find someone to take his place while it's still early."

Stefan felt like someone had kicked him in the stomach. Was that really the only reason he was cast? All those readings and talks with Mark and audition after audition.

"Sweetheart, it will all work out," Sherman said. "Stefan tested perfect; he's just nervous. He moves like a natural athlete, and he'll be great in the action scenes."

"Hello, you know I'm right here," Stefan said. He wondered if he had become invisible.

"I'm going to talk to Mark about this," Raine sniffled. "I'm sure Justin Seton is still available. He tested just as well, and they could do some makeup tricks to make him look more like me."

Raine's mother put her arm around her. "She's right. Get someone who can play the part."

"Mother, I'll handle this." Raine shrugged off the stained jacket and handed it to the costume designer, who made clucking noises at it before she scurried off, holding it in front of her.

Sherman glanced at Stefan and then turned his attention back to Raine. "It would cost quite a bit of money to bring in Justin Seton. Besides, once Stefan's character gets hurt and your character takes over, the movie is almost all yours from there on out. The final scene when Stefan comes back is split between the two of you, but you have the most important shots."

"I thought I just got a minor injury," Stefan said. Near the end of the script he got in a fight with one of the monster creatures on the planet, but it wasn't supposed to be serious.

"I was told Mark might change the script so Stefan's character dies," Raine said.

"Wait a minute!" Stefan protested. "Nobody ever said anything about me dying."

Sherman held up his hands. "Nothing has been decided. They're still working on the script. Mark likes to tinker with it as he goes along. You don't need to worry about that now."

"I don't want to die in the movie," Stefan said. How could he pull off some elaborate death scene? Did he even want to?

Sherman clapped him on the back. "I'm sure you can do it, if it comes to that. We'd make sure it's a spectacular, heroic kind of death. It will be great! What do you think, Raine?"

"Why don't you just have him trip over someone's foot and fall into a crevice," Raine's mother said. "I'm sure he could handle that."

That bit of nastiness silenced everyone for a few seconds. Stefan didn't know how to respond. If a kid had said that, he would have decked him.

"Mother! Stop! I'll talk to Mark when he gets back. Now I need to do my schoolwork. Why don't you go feed Mr. Snuggums? It's time for his snack."

Mrs. Randolph looked at her watch. "All right, but see that this gets settled. Come along, Mr. Snuggums. Poor baby. You must be famished!" Stefan was relieved to see her head up the stairs.

"It will all work out, Raine, I promise," Sherman said. "We'll make sure this movie showcases your extraordinary talent. We'll talk in the morning, okay? Take the night to relax." He ignored Stefan as he went out the front door.

Everyone else disappeared just as fast, until only Raine and Stefan were left.

"You look like a puppy someone has just kicked," Raine said. "Don't take it personally. It's business. If I don't look out for my career, no one else will."

"What about my career?" Not that he thought of this as a career. It was more a miracle out of nowhere to get the role, but the miracle would never turn into anything more if Raine got him fired.

"That's your problem, not mine. You better learn fast—it's everybody for themselves in this business. I'm so done with this day," she said, more to herself than to Stefan as she left the room.

He actually did feel like a kicked puppy. How could they change things on him this far into the game?

Stefan tried to make his face expressionless as he went into the room set aside for the costumes. He shouldn't have bothered. The costume people didn't even speak to him when he handed them his tunic. They were gathered around Raine's jacket, looking more like they were mourning at a funeral than staring at a piece of fabric. He grabbed his regular clothes and went into the changing room, trying not to listen to their discussion. It *was* just a piece of fabric, and he knew they had extras. After he was dressed, he tossed the rest of the costume on another table and left them to it.

Back in the lobby, he was unsure what to do.

Maybe he should quit the movie before he got fired. Tell them his mom needed him at home. Tell his mom he decided he didn't want to act. Except Heather would know the truth. He didn't remember what his contract said about quitting. If he quit, what would happen to the money he'd already been paid? It was spent, except the part that went into an account he couldn't get at until he was eighteen. The rest he couldn't give back.

"Stefan!" Heather came down the stairs in a cloud of perfume. "I'm going to dinner with Brad, you know, the wolf trainer? You're fine, right? Brad says he heard there's a fun pub in the village with live music, and I've been kind of bored hanging around here all day. Since you're going to be eating with Mark, you won't miss me, will you?"

Stefan looked out one of the windows. It had stopped snowing, but he wondered about the condition of the road down to village. "Are you sure you should drive on an unfamiliar road? Is Brad driving?" Heather was a terrible driver, even without snow. She'd been in so many accidents his mom didn't let any of them ride with her anymore.

"Stefan, you sound just like your mom. Who's the older one here? Just for your information,

Brad is driving, and there's a truck with a snow-plow attached to the front that's already headed down the mountain. Brad says one of the crew has been driving the truck back and forth all day, keeping the road clear. The village isn't that far away. I'm sure we'll be fine, and we'll be back in a few hours. Everyone is talking about how bad the snow will be tomorrow, and then we won't be able to go anywhere."

"If you get stuck, I'm going to tell you I told you so." His mom always said Heather couldn't sit still or be alone as a kid, wanting to be surrounded by people and noise all the time. He should have guessed she wouldn't want to hang around a quiet lodge.

"Is it okay if I take your cell phone with me? My battery is low. I hope you don't mind, I already picked up yours from your room."

Stefan suspected it was because she really wanted the charges to show up on his phone bill instead of hers. She was never one to spend money if she didn't have to. "Sure, have fun. Be careful."

"I will," she said, pulling up her coat around her neck. "Brad's waiting for me in the car."

After Heather left, Stefan went to the window

to check on the snow. Where the snow hadn't been shoveled it was deep, nice and smooth and unbroken. He wanted to be out in it, totally alone, away from everyone else. Sometimes at home he went out during a heavy snow, knowing everyone else would be inside, and he could let the cold air take over, clearing away everything crowding him.

Stefan ran upstairs and grabbed his coat. When he came back down he headed to the back door, right by the old reception desk. For some reason no one had been using the door, which meant he'd be less likely to run into anyone if he went out that way. When he opened it, he understood the reason it wasn't in use. There was a porch, but beyond that no one had shoveled the walkway to the parking lot. Stefan guessed it was just too much work to keep both the front and the back clear. Once he was outside the cold jolted him, but it was exactly what he wanted. The light was already fading, and he decided to get a closer look at the snow skimmers before it was completely dark. The set was so far away from any signs of civilization, the only lights he could see were the ones coming from the lodge and a few of the motor homes and the semitrailers. The rest looked like they had been shut up for the night.

He had to cross the parking lot to get to the far corner where the skimmers were located, and he was surprised to see something new on his way there. At some point during the afternoon someone had erected an igloo-shaped structure that looked like it had been carved out of pieces of black ice, ridged with abstract swirls. Stefan thought it might be the command outpost in the script. It was kind of bizarre looking, not exactly what he would have chosen, but at least it seemed futuristic. Whatever the designers had done to coat the thin metal panels that formed the building, they'd succeeded in creating an otherworldly look. There was a faint shimmer underneath the black, like the metal was glowing all on its own.

In the script, he crawled to the command outpost after he had been injured. If they made him die now, it would probably not happen there; more likely he would be doing something stupidly heroic. He still felt sick at the thought of having to do some big emotional scene he hadn't known about, like he was some puppet they could control by pulling the strings. Though if Raine had her way and he got fired, it wouldn't even be an issue.

All the more reason to look at the skimmers

while he could. When he reached them he ran his hand along the snow accumulating on the tarps. It would be nice to sit in one at least once. He checked behind him. The few remaining crew people across the parking lot were not paying any attention to him.

The tarps were fastened on with bungee cords, so it was easy to unhook one on the far side, out of sight. He shook off some of the snow and lifted up the corner to get a better look. The body of the skimmer was painted a metallic gray shade with the stylized wolf image on the side. There was one tube-like weapon mounted on each side, like rocket launchers. Stefan knew from the script there were supposed to be glove joysticks inside to control them, not to make them fire or anything, because they weren't real, but to make them move like they were being aimed. He took hold of one to see how far it would swing up and down, but it was fastened with some sort of temporary clamp, probably to hold it in place until they were ready for it. He unclamped it carefully and moved it up and down, picturing some sort of laser weapon shooting out of it.

The latch for the canopy was right in front of him. He clamped the tube weapon back on and then hesitated for a moment, eyeing the latch. It wouldn't have to be opened all the way for him to climb in. He'd just sit in it for a minute. He unlatched it.

The trailer made a perfect step to boost himself up. Once inside, Stefan realized too late the snow from his boots and his coat was getting all over. He didn't have any way to clean it up, so he hoped no one would notice. Closing his eyes, he put his hands into the joystick gloves and tried to visualize shooting at one of the many weird creatures in the script. Nothing came into his head, no image of flying or battling monsters or anything. How was he supposed to act scared of a prop? Maybe he was a lousy actor after all.

A man's voice right outside the skimmer said, "It's going to be a major job to get these rigged in all this snow." Stefan froze, hoping they didn't decide to lift the tarp. "I wish Mark would just take the easy way out and do this all in a warm, dry studio against a blue screen."

"Mark wants it more 'authentic.'" Another man gave a snort of disgust. "You know his reputation."

The voices moved off, and Stefan slumped down, relieved he didn't have to explain what he was doing. Being almost discovered took the fun out of sitting in the skimmer, so he waited a few minutes, trying to calculate how long it would take the men to walk away. When Stefan was sure they'd be gone, he lifted the canopy just enough to slip out, and fastened the tarp back down. The men hadn't been very observant; his footprints were everywhere in the snow. If the snow started again tomorrow, all traces of his presence would be gone soon enough. He shivered, deciding it was time to head inside. Maybe everyone else would be so busy they wouldn't notice him. He didn't think he could take any more death glares about Raine's costume.

Crossing the parking lot to get to the back door, Stefan smelled pipe smoke, spicy and sweet at the same time, like a mix of smoke and cherries. It reminded him of his grandfather. Before his death, his grandfather smoked a pipe almost every evening, and the scent of it was a signal that the day was ending in a good way.

The scent was coming across the lot from one of the semitrailers. Stefan hadn't yet been in any of them, but they looked like they were specially adapted for movie use. Unlike normal semis, these all had trailers on the back that reminded

Stefan of office buildings on wheels, with doors on one side and portable steps pushed up to them. As he drew closer to the pipe smell, he could see a sliver of light shining out from one of the doors. It opened all the way, and Cecil came out onto the top step, tapping his pipe on the frame. Stefan held still, not wanting the old man to notice him, but Cecil did. "Stefan? Is that you under all that snow? What are you doing standing out in the cold?" He opened the door and motioned. "Come join us! There's someone you should meet."

Stefan couldn't figure out a way to say no, but once inside he was glad he had come in. The place looked like a high-tech Santa's workshop. It was jammed with tools. Cables crisscrossed the room, connecting multiple laptops, and bits of unidentifiable creatures were scattered about, including one supersized furry paw that ended in teeth instead of claws. There was hardly room to move.

"Come on in," a voice said. "I'm almost finished here."

"Stefan, meet the finest creature designer in the world, Alan McKellon," Cecil said. "He's the real star of these movies." The man who looked up from a keyboard fit the room. He was like Santa

Claus turned pirate, beads braided into his white fluffy beard and one large hoop earring glinting in the light.

Cecil moved a chair out the way so he could close the door. "I was ecstatic when I heard Alan was on board. You should have seen the creatures he made for my last movie, *They Came From Below*. Did you ever catch that?"

Stefan shook his head. "No, sorry."

"I guess I'm not surprised." Cecil sighed. "It went straight to DVD anyway. The lead actor turned out to be abysmal. I should have done the zombie movie instead. Mr. McKellon, why don't you amaze and astound this young gentleman with some of your creations?"

"He's already seen one of them. What did you think of my frost devils? I worked very hard to get the color of the intestines just right."

So no one had told McKellon what had happened. "They were . . . great," Stefan said. "Very alien looking."

"Good! Good! I want you to see some of my other lovelies." McKellon pulled out what looked sort of like a softball-sized crystal spider, except it had dozens of legs instead of just eight. "I've had myself a grand time with these. They'll be the ones popping up out of the snow and coating the unwary with ice threads. According to the script, they work in packs, like piranhas. I believe some of your loyal followers will meet a rather unfortunate demise." He put the spider on his sleeve and squeezed the top of it, which made its legs clamp down on his arm. "Not very cuddly, are they?"

"Do they really spit out ice threads?" Stefan asked.

"Sorry, lad, they don't really do that. That effect will be added in postproduction. They do make an unpleasant sound though. Listen to this." He pushed a hidden button, and the ice spider let out a high-pitched buzzing noise, like giant wasps, overlaid with a screeching metal-scraping-on-metal sound. Stefan covered his ears.

"I would describe that as appalling rather than merely unpleasant," Cecil said.

"When they're all going, it's enough to drive a chap insane." McKellon sounded cheerful at the idea. "And I've finally got these working." He picked up a costume that looked identical to the one Stefan had just taken off, holding it out. Stefan took it, surprised at how heavy it was.

"What's different about this one?" Stefan asked.

"Mark had a rather last-minute idea that the

disks on your costumes are supposed to activate to form your own personal shield armor, like a force field. The costumes you'll wear for most of the shots don't have the hardware sewn into them, because it's easily damaged, but for certain shots you'll wear these." McKellon reached into the end of one sleeve, and immediately each disk let out a circular glow, overlapping all the others.

"The disks were made so that we could embed hundreds of LED lights and connect them to battery packs. I'm afraid these tunics will be much heavier than your regular ones, but at least they'll be warmer, too. Good for this location, not so good once you're on the studio set."

"These are really great!" Stefan said, thinking how amazing it would be if the lights actually worked like real shields. Maybe someday in the future that sort of thing would be invented.

"I'm still working out this one. It's for your stunt double when he falls off the cliff, and I don't want the battery packs to hurt him when he hits the air bag at the bottom."

Stefan went still. "I fall off a cliff?"

McKellon laughed. "Not you! I said it was your double. And he'll fall right onto a nice cushioned air bag." The prop man pointed at some rolls of black plastic lined up neatly on a shelf behind him. "They don't look like much now, but when we blow them up, it's just like falling into the softest mattress you can imagine."

That wasn't what Stefan meant, but he didn't correct McKellon. The script he had seen didn't have any cliff falls. He knew he was going to have a stunt double, because he wasn't old enough to be allowed to do his own stunts, but he didn't know they had added that into the script. Was that the death scene?

"I wish I had time to show you the larger creature costumes." Alan switched off the lights on the tunic. "They're in the other trailer, but imagine something like a gigantic bear with a saber-toothed baboon face covered in a rather ghastly walrus hide instead of fur. Fantastically frightening. We've hired some very, very tall extras to wear them. It's getting late, and about time to close up, so I'll have to show them to you tomorrow."

Stefan wasn't sure he'd still be here. If he was, he'd bring Jeremy along. The kid would probably like to see them.

"Where are you staying?" Cecil asked Alan. "I

thought I'd nip into the village one night for a meal."

"The rest of the props team and I are at one of the more remote hotels. They've scattered us across twelve villages to find enough rooms for us all. How's the lodge fitted out for you? I'm surprised they went to so much trouble to get it in shape."

"They did it so the children wouldn't waste their limited working time on being driven back and forth to the set. We're on a tight schedule as it is. I quite like being right here. Not such an early call in the mornings. And there won't be any late-night noise from the neighbors. I don't think there's a soul within miles of us."

"There may be no call at all tomorrow if the snow starts up again." McKellon checked his watch. "Time to go."

Outside, Stefan flipped his collar up around his neck trying to block the cold. He was ready to be back inside.

"You did fine today," Cecil said to him. "The first days of filming are always rough."

"Right." Stefan knew Cecil was just trying to make him feel better. He doubted if many first days went as badly as this one had.

"Why don't you go on ahead, Stefan?" Cecil said. "I want a few more words with Alan."

Stefan headed back to the lodge, wondering what he was going to do with himself when he got there. When he came in he almost ran into Jeremy's dad, who was standing by the front door, wearing a coat and boots. He nodded to Stefan but then turned away like he wasn't planning to talk to him.

Stefan heard Raine's mother's voice in the upstairs hallway. "It's good for your acting to be stuck here. My acting coach used to tell me to work with my emotions. This place is perfect for that. You're supposed to feel cut off from everything, and you really are!"

"Next job I'm staying at a five-star hotel, no matter what," Raine answered. Stefan wondered if she'd get that put in her contract too. He felt weird eavesdropping, but he didn't want to go upstairs and have to speak to them.

"Fine." Raine's mother sounded like she wasn't even listening anymore. "Mark made it clear I didn't need to be at dinner with all of you. I can take a hint. Jeremy's father invited me to the restaurant in the village, so we'll leave you all to work out the problem with Stefan."

Stefan heard the sound of heels clicking down the stairs, so he ducked into the empty office room. There was a narrow staircase at one end. He went up it as quietly as possible, pausing to make sure the coast was clear. So what if he was being a big chicken? A person could only take so much in one day. Back in his room, he dropped onto the bed, so tired he couldn't even think straight.

When he woke up, the lodge was quiet, very quiet, like the snow had muted everything and everyone. The silence didn't seem right; he could tell from the faint light coming in the window it wasn't that late. People should still be working, but when he looked outside, most of the vehicles were gone from the parking lot. He could see one car in the distance, slowly making its way down the winding road, the taillights like two red eyes barely visible in the swirling snow.

Someone knocked on his door. "Stefan, it's Jeremy. Are you there? Can I come in?" Jeremy sounded panicked.

Stefan opened the door, and Jeremy almost fell into the room.

"You're still here!"

"Where else would I be?" Stefan rubbed his

eyes, feeling groggy.

"The lodge is empty! My dad said I was sup-posed to stay in the room and do my homework until six o'clock and then go eat dinner with Mark and you. I just went downstairs and there's nobody here. Everyone's disappeared!"

Chapter 8

ECHOES

"I'm scared," Jeremy said. "It's really creepy here with nobody around."

"Somebody has to be around." Stefan rubbed his eyes, trying to clear the fog in his head. "There were fifty people here a little while ago. I know your dad went into town, but where's Amanda?"

"She went to her hotel. She doesn't have to stay with us once we're done for the day. Our parents are supposed to be in charge then."

Stefan stuck his head out into the hallway. All the doors were closed. "Did you knock on anybody else's door?"

"No, I didn't want anyone to get mad at me for bothering them."

Stefan wasn't quite sure what to do. He knew all the rooms on the floor had been renovated for them, but he hadn't figured out who was in what room. There were nine in all, one each for him, Heather, Raine, her mother, Mark, the assistant director, the producer, and Jeremy and his dad in a room together. He didn't know who, if anyone, was staying on the third floor.

Jeremy twisted his hands together. "I heard a noise downstairs near the dining room but I was scared to go look. There weren't any voices, just rattling noises, like chains. Do you think there are ghosts here?"

"Don't be silly." Stefan checked his watch. "It's only five thirty. I don't think a ghost would be out roaming around now. Maybe people are in their rooms just resting. Let's go downstairs and see if we can find someone."

It was a little eerie walking down the silent hallway; no sounds, not even the drone of a television, came from any of the rooms. Raine was supposed to be here, but Stefan didn't really want to knock on the doors like he was looking for her.

When they went down the stairs, there was no one in the lobby. The dining room, lit only by one dim chandelier and candles, was empty, although food was laid out on a long table. The room could have been a movie set too, some medieval fantasy movie where people gnawed on turkey legs in a huge hall. There were no sounds of rattling chains, but there was a giant stone fireplace at one end with a snarling wolf head mounted on a shield above it and faded tapestries on the walls.

"That wolf head is scary, isn't it?" Jeremy said. "Though it's really mean they did that to a wolf. This place is kind of spooky, don't you think?" He pointed up to the exposed rafters in the ceiling. "I thought I saw something move up there at lunch."

"It's probably just a mouse. I'm sure the place is crawling with them," Stefan said, "since it's been shut up so long." He could just imagine how many mice could have taken up residence in such a huge old place. They waged a constant battle with them at their house, and they had a cat to help. A clanging noise came from behind a door at the end of the room.

"See," Jeremy whispered. "What's that?"

Before Stefan could answer, the door opened and a small, round woman in an apron came out with a huge platter. She smiled when she saw them and said something not in English.

So much for a ghost. Stefan hadn't realized he'd been holding his breath until he relaxed at the sight of the woman. "Hi," he said. "I'm sorry, I don't speak . . . whatever language that is. Slovakian?"

The woman set the tray down with the rest of the food and gestured toward it, still talking and smiling.

"It all looks great," Stefan said to her. "I think she wants us to eat." He was starving, and the food smelled really good, but he didn't know if it was okay just to start eating.

"Do you think we should go ahead?" Jeremy asked.

"Yes," Stefan said. "When Mark gets back, we'll just eat again."

Stefan couldn't really name most of the food. There were bowls of dumplings, and potatoes in a sauce, and different kinds of meats on platters. Several of the dishes were topped with bacon, so he filled his plate with those, figuring anything with bacon had to be good.

"I wish it wasn't so dark in here," Jeremy said. "I still think it's creepy."

"It just needs some more lights." There were candles on all the tables, so Stefan set his plate down to grab a few. He put them on the table right under the chandelier, where there was the most light, and retrieved his plate. Too hungry to wait for Jeremy, he took a bite. Whatever it was, it tasted good, kind of like spicy fried chicken, except he wasn't sure it was chicken.

Jeremy brought his plate over the table just as Raine came into the room carrying her dog. Stefan knew he couldn't avoid her forever, but he really wished she had stayed away a few more minutes until he was finished.

"Where is everybody?" she asked. "Weren't we going to eat with Mark?"

"He's not back yet and we got hungry," Jeremy said.

"Oh. I guess I'll wait for him. I have a lot of studying to do." Raine didn't look very excited at the prospect.

"Eat with us," Jeremy said. "We've decided we'll eat again when Mark gets back. And it's not like Amanda's going to give you a detention if you don't finish your homework."

"Well, I guess I can have something." Raine put Mr. Snuggums down on a chair and then went over to the serving table. The only thing she came back with was a bowl of some sort of brownish soup.

"Do you know how few vitamins are on that plate?" She pointed at Jeremy's plate as she sat down. Stefan hadn't noticed it was piled high with bread, potatoes, and desserts.

"No," Jeremy said. "How few?"

"Basically there are no vitamins on that plate. You should get at least one healthy thing."

"I don't like food that has colors in it," Jeremy said, "except pizza and dessert. Anyway, potatoes are vegetables, right?" Jeremy took a big piece of bread and slathered butter on it and then dipped it in some potatoes. Raine gave a snort of disgust.

"What are *you* eating?" Jeremy asked her. "It looks bad."

"For your information, it's lentil soup and it's delicious."

There was an awkward silence after that. So much for the whole family idea. Mr. Snuggums sat perfectly still, eyeing Stefan's plate intently. Stefan thought the dog looked glum, but then he'd be glum too if he had to wear a fuzzy green sweater with a moose on it.

"How many outfits does Mr. Snuggums have?" Jeremy asked.

"I don't know. My mom likes to buy them. She's the one who changes his clothes all the time. It keeps her busy and out of my hair. And you don't have to call him Mr. Snuggums. That's just my mom's silly name for him. His real name on his pedigree is Horizon's Namcha Barwa."

"That's better?" Stefan asked. Was she joking?

"Pedigreed dogs always have long names. I call him Kep when my mom's not around. You can too if you want. Did you ever read . . ." Her face turned red as she cut off her sentence.

"Kep's good," Stefan said, not understanding why she was blushing.

"It's the name of a collie in a kid's book I used to like. I know he's not much like a collie, but he's a good dog."

"Does Mr. Snuggums, I mean Kep, always breathe so funny?" Jeremy asked. "It sounds like he has asthma too."

"I think it's because his face is all smushed in," Stefan said. "Nothing could breathe well like that." He kind of felt sorry for the dog, moose sweater and all. And it was easier to like the animal if he could stop thinking of him as Mr. Snuggums.

"He's a pug," Raine said. "That's the way they breathe."

Kep put his chin on the table, and Jeremy patted his head. "If I wasn't allergic to dogs, I'd like a golden retriever."

"I'd like one too," Raine said, "but I can't exactly carry a golden retriever around under my arm on set."

More silence. Stefan bit into something that turned out to be a giant plum dumpling. It was heaven. After he finished, he started on the other dessert. "I don't know what these thin pancakes with the chocolate are called, but they're great."

"They're crêpes," Raine said, rolling her eyes like he was an idiot for not knowing that. "You've just consumed about a pound of sugar."

"So?" He was getting fed up with her. So what if she was a famous movie star. "Who made you the diet police? What are you, some mini-adult disguised as a kid?"

"Fine," Raine snapped. "Eat what you want. I don't really care anyway."

"Fine." Stefan picked up the last crêpe and ate it in one big bite.

There were more moments of silence and then Jeremy said, "I wonder if Cecil is going to eat. He's supposed to be here."

Raine shuddered. "He gives me the creeps."

"I think he's nice," Jeremy said. "My dad told me he used to be famous."

"Don't you know about him?" Raine spoke in a

low voice, her gaze darting around like she was expecting people to overhear.

Jeremy's fork stopped halfway to his mouth. "No . . . what about him?"

She leaned in toward them and said, "Most of the movies he's worked on were cursed."

"How can a movie be cursed?" Stefan scoffed.

"It happens." Raine nodded her head like she was agreeing with herself. "Either people get hurt or weird, spooky things happen. I heard it started way back on the first movies he worked on. Every set had more than their share of accidents, and after one movie, both the director and the lead actor *died* before the movie was released. They think it was because the movie was about an ancient Egyptian curse and they used a real sarcophagus, a cursed one, in the movie."

Jeremy let out a little gasp.

"I don't believe anybody could use an actual sarcophagus," Stefan argued. "Those are only in museums and they don't loan them out. What does that have to do with Cecil anyway?"

"He was the mummy in the movie!" Raine said, as if that explained anything. "And then he starred in *The Cave of Blood*. I heard the actors would find little drops of real blood all over the set in weird places. And right near the end of filming, a stuntman was found dead in the prop coffin one morning when they unlocked the soundstage." Her voice dropped almost to a whisper. "They never solved the murder."

"That's awful!" Jeremy whispered back. "Do they think Cecil did it?"

Oh great, Stefan thought. He wished Raine would stop talking. With his luck, Jeremy would be the type to have bad dreams. The kid's room was right next to his.

"Are you sure?" Stefan asked. "This all sounds like one of those urban legends. How do you know all this?"

"Everybody in Hollywood knows." From Raine's tone, he could tell she was angry at him for questioning her. "That's one of the reasons he hardly ever gets work anymore. He hasn't done a film in five years. For some insane reason, Mark has a soft spot for him because he grew up watching Cecil's horror movies."

"He was just acting in them, you know, because he's like . . . an actor," Stefan said.

"Don't you think it's weird he chose to be in those movies? I almost backed out when I heard he was hired for this movie, but my mom said we needed the money for a new house. If terrible things start to happen though, I'm gone."

Just then Cecil shuffled into the room, looking really tired. "Rather a slow night tonight at Chez Location restaurant," he said to them, using a very exaggerated British accent. He straightened up and surveyed the room, acting like he was adjusting an imaginary bow tie. "I see I shall easily get the best table in the house without needing to tip the maître d'. I hope the service isn't overly slow."

Stefan was relieved when Jeremy laughed, like he hadn't really believed Raine's crazy stories. There was still a bit of chocolate sauce on Stefan's plate so he scraped it up with his fork, trying to decide if he wanted more.

After Cecil sat down with his own plate, Jeremy blurted out, "I know you used to be famous because my dad told me so. Did you ever get to meet Daniel Radcliffe when you were?" Stefan suppressed a groan. If Jeremy had been one of his brothers, he would have kicked him under the table to let him know that wasn't a polite thing to say. Jeremy kept talking, not noticing the stillness that had fallen over the table. "I wish I'd been old enough to audition for a Harry Potter movie."

Cecil's expression flattened out for a few seconds and then he said, "No, sorry. I've never had the pleasure of meeting Mr. Radcliffe. And your father is right. I was famous. Once. Would you like to see one of my best tricks?" He turned away from them for a few seconds, and when he turned back, Jeremy let out a yell. Kep growled, and Stefan had to clench his teeth shut to avoid yelping himself. Cecil's hair hung in thin gray strands, his eyes bulging out. He hunched over, one side of his mouth twisted up in a sneer, his hands held out like claws. It was as if they were watching some hideous creature crawling out of a grave.

"Wow, how did you do that?" Stefan asked. "Can you teach me?"

Cecil relaxed back to his normal self, pushing his hair back into place. "Only some of it. The eyes are just something I have always been able to do. You have to be born with the ability, if you want to call it that." He took a couple of bites of bread and then pushed the plate away. "I don't think I'm very hungry after all. These old bones need to get to bed because jet lag is setting in. Tomorrow I will help you begin to tame the planet, but tonight I need my wool blanket."

The cook came out of the kitchen talking away,

pointing first at the table, then making eating motions. Stefan said, "I'm sorry, we don't understand." The woman threw up her hands and went back into the kitchen.

"I suspect she wants to clean up. If you want anything else, I'd get it now." Cecil got up, and Stefan was surprised at how much older the man suddenly looked. "Good night, children." He moved off slowly and Stefan heard him say, "'And all the rest forgot for which he toil'd,'" like he was talking to himself.

The wind howled in the fireplace, stirring up some ancient ashes and rattling the windows. Stefan could see it had started to snow again. The flakes were blowing against the panes so hard it was like they were pelting them. With Cecil gone, the room grew much emptier.

"What did I tell you?" Raine said. "He's bizarre."

"*I* like him," Stefan said.

"What's that noise?" Jeremy stood up and glanced around. "It sounds like howling."

"I don't hear anything," Raine said. "I wonder why no one else is eating. They must be about done putting things away."

"Almost everyone else is staying in town," Jeremy said. "Mark told my dad it was too expensive to refit the whole lodge, so they just fixed up the rooms on the second floor and a few on the third for us and some of the crew."

Stefan was about to say he needed more dessert when a banging sound and then the howl of a wolf cut him off. The weirdest thing about the sound was that it seemed to echo inside the building.

Jeremy went over to the window that looked out onto the ski slope. "The door to the wolves' motor home is opening and shutting! It must have come unlocked. And it's all dark in there."

Stefan joined him. "I'm not sure there were any lights on in the first place. It's not like wolves need a night-light." Another wolf started to howl and the sound echoed above them, except it wasn't really an echo, because it came out at the same time.

"Am I the only one who thinks it sounds like the wolves are inside the lodge?" Raine asked.

So it wasn't just him. "Maybe it's something to do with the storm. You know sound travels in weird ways."

"I don't think it travels like that, up the stairs and into a room above us. Do you think some wolves got inside?" Raine asked.

"They can't get inside," Stefan said. "It's not like they can open the front door. They're smart but not that smart. And why would a wolf come inside and go up to the third floor?"

"How do you know what a wolf would or wouldn't do?'

A louder howl came from both outside and above their heads.

"That's not my imagination," Raine said.

Chapter 9

NIGHTFALL

"What if it's that wolf Stefan saw this morning?" Jeremy said, his voice wavering. "What if it sneaked inside earlier and it's been hiding here all day? There are lots of empty rooms upstairs."

Jeremy sounded exactly like Stefan's brothers whenever he was babysitting them. They were sure the instant his mom closed the door behind her, all the hidden monsters were going to pop out. He always had to take action fast before they scared themselves silly. "I'll prove there're no wolves inside." Stefan pointed in the direction of the lobby. "Come on, let's go look."

"I'm not staying here by myself!" Raine said.

The three of them walked out of the dining

room and paused at the bottom of the central staircase. "I don't hear anything now." Stefan tried to sound optimistic.

"It's only been a few seconds," Jeremy said.

When they reached the second floor, it was completely empty and silent except for a faint snore coming from what Stefan assumed was Cecil's door. Raine made a face at it. Stefan hadn't noticed before, but the hall smelled like Cecil's pipe tobacco and pine. It was a good smell, not the least bit spooky.

The staircase to the third floor was at one end of the hallway. It was much narrower than the main one, the boards so worn down they sagged in the middle. "I hope somebody checked these out," Stefan said, worrying the wood was rotten.

"I'll go first." Raine moved in front of him and started creeping slowly up the stairs. They creaked but held. She stopped and looked back at them, beaming. "This is so great! I feel just like Nancy Drew! I wish I'd brought a flashlight. On the cover of *The Hidden Staircase*, she has a flashlight to light the way."

And Raine was the one who thought Cecil bizarre. "Um . . . okay . . . Can we keep going, Nancy?" Stefan said.

A noise, like scratching or skittering, came from above them before anyone could answer Stefan.

"There's something up there," Raine whispered.

"It's mice, I'm sure," Stefan spoke as loud as he could. "You don't need to whisper. They know we're here."

Another faint howl echoed down the stairs.

"I didn't know mice could howl," Raine said. "Unless they are werewolf mice. Or I guess they would just be called weremice. You know, that might make a great story!"

The image of tiny shaggy mice with ferocious teeth wasn't something Stefan needed to think about. "Raine, can we concentrate and keep going?"

At the top of the stairs the scent of tobacco and pine disappeared, replaced by a musty smell, and the odor of . . . of peanut butter. The skittering sounds came from one room about midway down. The door was ajar, a light shining from it. As they started toward it, a white shape burst out and glided silently down the hall away from them, disappearing into the last room at the end.

"It's a ghost!" Jeremy screamed, clutching Stefan's arm.

"It's an owl," Stefan said, after he got his voice back. "They don't make any noise when they fly. I bet it lives in here just like barn owls live in barns, catching mice. I told you the place would be crawling with them."

"Wow! An owl in a hotel!" Raine exclaimed. "This is going to make a great story to tell reporters! I want to see what's in that room. Maybe there's a nest."

Inside the room were two open duffel bags on the floor and a jumble of clothes. The peanut butter smell came from a tipped-over open jar of peanut butter on the nightstand. Peanut butter mouse tracks made a path across the table and down to the floor.

"There's where the noise is coming from." Stefan pointed at a receiver on the dresser. "It's a sound monitor. The other part must be in the wolves' motor home so the trainers can hear what's going on. This is the trainers' room."

Another howl came from the monitor. Jeremy crossed over to the window. "Why do you think they are howling? Maybe something is wrong."

Stefan joined him, not able to remember if there had been any lights on earlier in the motor home. It was completely dark now. He could just make out the door, swinging back and forth in the wind. Every once in a while a particularly strong gust would push it against the side of the vehicle, and each time it hit, one of the wolves howled.

"They sound really unhappy. Why isn't the wolf handler taking care of it? Isn't he out there with them?" Raine asked.

"No. He went into town with my aunt to have dinner."

"They left the wolves here all alone?" Jeremy said.

"I think wolves can take care of themselves. They've been doing it for thousands of years."

"These wolves are locked in cages. How are they supposed to take care of themselves?" Jeremy sounded indignant.

"It's not like the handlers sleep in there with them anyway. You've seen the place. It's as nice in there as it is in here."

"Maybe they're upset because Inky isn't there. Someone needs to go out and fasten the door," Raine said. "So they don't get cold."

They both looked at Stefan. "Good idea," he said. "Raine, why don't you go?"

"I didn't mean me. I want to get back to studying."

"I'll go with you," Jeremy said.

Stefan sighed. He knew the wolves wouldn't stop howling with the door banging. "Okay, but we're just fastening the door and leaving. It's really cold out."

"Great! I want to get my flashlight first." Jeremy ran out of the room, and Stefan wondered why he sounded so excited about going out in the cold and the dark.

Raine walked over to the window. "I think this is what they call a real blizzard now. Look how the wind is blowing. You should tie yourselves together with ropes so you don't get lost. I read that in a book once, *Little House on the Prairie*, I think. You can get lost just a few feet from your own door and freeze to death. Maybe I'll go with you after all." For some reason she sounded thrilled at the idea of braving the storm. "Where do we get some rope?" She ran to the hallway like she was expecting to find a hardware store there.

"Raine, I'm sure we can make it out and back long before you could find enough rope. We're not out on the prairie. Why don't you stand at the door and yell for us if it looks like we're getting lost?"

This satisfied her, but once Stefan and Jeremy left the lodge, Stefan wished they had followed her idea. The wind sliced into him, blasting so much snow at his face he could only see a few feet in front of him. Jeremy grabbed onto his coat and buried his own face in the fabric of Stefan's. It was really dark. The only illumination came from the windows of the lodge, and they were already getting snow-covered again, so that they glowed very faintly, like candles almost spent. The motor home seemed so much farther away than Stefan remembered.

When they finally reached it, the door had slammed shut, and Stefan had to wrench it back open. Inside, he groped for the switch, but when he moved it up and down, nothing happened.

"Why aren't the lights going on?" Jeremy asked.

"The power's out. A line from the main building to here is probably down." Stefan hadn't noticed one on the walk out here, and it made him very nervous to think of a live power line hidden somewhere under the snow. The place was already freezing, so Stefan pulled the door closed after them.

Jeremy shone his flashlight around the room and it reflected off the eyes of the wolves as it passed over them. They were all sitting upright by the doors of their cages, except for Phoebe, who was gnawing on the latch. Natasha growled when she saw them.

"We'll have to take them inside with us," Jeremy said. "They'll get too cold out here, don't you think?"

"They won't get too cold. We'll just shut the door. They have fur coats and they *are* wolves. Regular wolves live outside in the winter." Their glowing eyes made Stefan uneasy. The animals looked wilder and bigger in the dark.

"But these aren't regular wolves. We can't leave them out here. It's up to us to take care of them."

"Jeremy, I'm not the guy here who gets to decide stuff." Stefan didn't want to get into any more trouble. After hurting one wolf, what would they say if he let the others out?

"You're the oldest here, I mean besides Cecil, and he's sleeping, and the cook, and she doesn't speak English. It's just like in our movie—because no one else is here, you're in charge."

"This isn't the movie, though, and people will be back in a few hours. What if they run off?"

"We'll put leashes on them!"

Stefan could tell the kid wasn't going to give

up. A tremendous burst of wind shook the vehicle so hard, it tilted to one side. Boris barked and the other two wolves wagged their tails excitedly. Phoebe reached her nose up to the wire of the cage.

"What if the motor home tips over?" Jeremy asked.

"I don't know if it can tip over." He didn't want to find out, but maybe it would be better to take the wolves inside. Maybe Hans would forgive him for hurting Inky if he took care of these wolves. He hesitated, unsure which was the best choice. When the motor home swayed again he made a decision. "Okay, I guess we can't leave them out here."

They opened the cage doors. Boris and Phoebe came out, but Natasha refused. She stood at the back of the cage, a low rumble coming from her throat.

"Let's go," Stefan said to her, swinging her door open as wide as possible. The rumble grew louder.

"Or let's not go." He took his hand away from the door slowly.

"We can't just leave her here."

"I'm not going to reach in there and get bitten. We'll just leave. Maybe she'll follow Boris." He snapped a leash on Boris's collar and then turned to Phoebe. She shrank away from him. "I'm not coming after you," he said to the wolf. "You'll have to make up your own mind." He still felt uncomfortable treating them exactly like dogs. Even dogs would bite if you tried to force them to do something they didn't want to.

When he tried to open the door to the outside, he couldn't. It felt like someone was standing outside pushing against it.

"Here, take Boris's leash," Stefan said, handing the end to Jeremy. He braced his foot more firmly on the floor and used both hands to shove on the door. It opened a few inches and then the wind caught it, blowing it open and banging it against the outside wall again. Wind and snow rushed in, and Stefan fell back. The storm was a frenzy now. He could see a wall of swirling white outside, but he couldn't see the lodge anymore. It was unbelievable.

"Jeremy, I think we should stay here until the storm calms down." The motor home rocked to one side, and Stefan had to grab the door frame to keep his balance. He could hear one of the wolves slipping across the floor, its toenails scraping against the linoleum. The door slammed shut.

"We can't! What if the whole thing tips over?" Jeremy sounded panicky.

Stefan didn't know what to do. Even if the vehicle was stable enough, could they spend the night here with no lights and no heat? The motor home shifted again and Jeremy made a noise like a sob.

That decided it. "Okay, we'll go. I'll get the door open again and then hold it so it won't hit the wolves. You lead Boris out." He handed the leash to Jeremy. "Just walk in the direction of the lodge and we'll be able to see it soon." He hoped that was true, and that people didn't really get lost in blizzard just a few feet from safety. Stefan was ready for the door this time. He grabbed hold and shoved out just enough. When he felt the wind grab the door he went with it, out into the cold. The door hit against the side of the motor home, and Stefan flung himself flat against it, pushing his feet hard against the step.

"Go, Jeremy!" When Jeremy stepped out, Stefan thought the wind was going to knock the boy over, but Jeremy bent down and shuffled forward. Boris followed him, and Stefan was relieved to see Phoebe edge forward. She paused at the entrance and looked out into the whiteness. Jeremy had stopped and was looking back.

"Keep moving!" Stefan yelled over the wind.

When Jeremy and Boris had taken a few steps toward the lodge, Phoebe launched herself out the door after them, catching up quickly. Stefan peered back into the dark of the motor home. He couldn't see Natasha. "I'm not waiting for you," he said, feeling silly for talking to a wolf. Her head appeared, and then the rest of her. She didn't even glance at Stefan; she just bent her head to go after the others. He saw Jeremy fall and flounder in the snow, so he let go of the door and jumped off the steps.

Once he was out in the full force of the wind, he felt like he was trying to walk through solid air. He figured out a bent-over shuffling motion that helped him keep his balance, but each step took a concentrated effort. When he got to Jeremy, he reached down and hauled the boy up. Jeremy was shaking, one hand clutched to Boris's fur.

"It's only a little farther!" Stefan thought he could make out a light from the lodge though the snow was caking his eyelashes so much he could hardy keep his eyes open. Grasping Jeremy's arm with one hand he practically dragged him back to the lodge, while trying not to step on Boris, who was pressed against his other side.

Luckily, Raine was waiting to open the door wide enough for them, so Stefan gave one last boost to Jeremy and pushed him through, collapsing next to him on the rug. Boris and Phoebe crowded in after them. Natasha stood for a moment outside like she was debating whether or not to enter, but she finally slunk in, keeping close to the wall. Raine slammed the door shut.

Stefan lay for a minute trying to get his breath.

"I didn't think it was going to be that hard for you," Raine said, her voice shaky. "I was about ready to come out and help." She helped Jeremy up and began to brush the snow off of him.

"That was really scary!" Jeremy said. "But it was worth it. We rescued the wolves!"

Stefan sat up and pulled off his boots, rubbing his numb feet. He thought Boris was the only wolf who looked pleased to be "rescued." Phoebe was crouched as close as she could to the door, and Natasha nosed at the door handle like she wanted it to open.

"We're not opening that door for you," he said to her.

"What do we do now?" Jeremy asked. "The wolves seem really nervous."

"Why don't we just sit down and act normal, so the wolves will relax," Raine suggested.

The cook walked out of the dining room and shrieked in surprise, backing up and then peeking around the corner of the door frame. She gestured at them and the wolves, jabbering away.

"It's okay," Stefan said, even though he knew she wouldn't understand. "They're tame." He tried to smile reassuringly. How do you pantomime a tame wolf? He made patting motions with his hands and then realized how ridiculous that looked.

The cook continued to talk. She pointed to the library, then pointed at the wolves, making sweeping motions with her hands.

"She wants us to put them in there," Raine said.

"It's probably not a bad idea," Stefan said. "People will freak out when they get back here tonight and find a wolf lounging on the rug." The cook threw her hands in the air and disappeared back into the dining room.

"I don't think anyone's getting back here tonight," Raine said, holding up her phone. "Mark, my mom, and Jeremy's dad all called. Don't either of you have your phones with you?"

Jeremy patted at his pockets. "I guess it's in my room. I forget to carry it around. Did my dad sound mad?"

"No. He just wanted to make sure you were okay. And now my mom called and said there was an accident on the bridge right outside the village. They think the bridge might be damaged and they're not letting anyone across it right away. They have to wait until morning to see how much damage there is. There's no other way up here." Raine smiled.

"Does Mark know there's no one here but us and Cecil and the cook?" Jeremy asked.

"No, he called first, and when I talked to him I thought the parental types were coming back tonight so I didn't tell him. And there was no way I was telling my mom."

"Maybe we should call my dad," Jeremy said. "We can't be here by ourselves."

"We're not by ourselves. What can they do anyway? If they can't get across the bridge how are they supposed to get here? We're fine." Raine laughed. "I stay at home with just a housekeeper all the time. And she's so busy watching television, she wouldn't notice if I left for a few days.

It's great when you think about it. We're snow-bound!" She twirled around. "No one to bother us!"

"But they'll be worried, don't you think, Ste-fan?"

"No they won't," Raine answered for him. "I didn't tell him you were out collecting wolves. It's usually better not to let adults know things that will worry them. There's no point in getting every-one all crazy. You do not want to see my mother in one of her lunatic modes."

"What about your aunt, Stefan? Won't she be worried?" Jeremy asked.

Stefan doubted if Heather had given much thought to him, and his mom would have no reason to call back in the next few hours. "No, Heather won't worry, and no one should try to drive in this anyway. It's snowing way too hard now."

Raine's phone rang. "Hello?" she said. "I can't hear you very well." After a few seconds she handed the phone to Stefan. "It's your aunt."

Sometimes Heather surprised him. "Hi, Heather?" There was music blasting in the back-ground.

"Stefan," Heather yelled. "I heard we can't get

back tonight. Everything okay?"

He hesitated. Raine was right. What good would it do to worry people?

"Everything's fine."

"What?" she yelled.

"FINE! I'll see you in the morning."

"We should at least tell Cecil," Jeremy said.

"No, don't wake him up," Raine said. "What can he do? It's not like he's going to make us hot chocolate and read us a bedtime story. He'd be more likely to tell us a gruesome horror story, and I'm not in the mood for one."

"I'm really tired and cold," Stefan said. "Let's put the wolves in the library and call it a night. By the time we wake up, the storm will probably be done, and everything will get back to normal." He didn't wait for an answer; he just picked up Boris's leash and led the wolf to the library. He was thankful the others followed, because he didn't have a plan if they didn't.

After he shut the door on them, a howl sounded outside.

"Was that the wind?" Raine asked.

"No. If we have all the wolves in here, then what's howling outside?" Jeremy asked, his voice trembling.

"Wild wolves," Stefan said. He knew it hadn't been just a dog behind the craft service truck. "They probably heard our wolves howling." Jeremy looked scared again, so Stefan tried to reassure him. "But they're a long way away outside. We're here inside a lodge. They aren't going to bother us."

"Good thing we're inside." Raine went over to a window and pushed on the glass. "I hope these are strong. I read this book where wolves threw themselves at the window of a train and broke through to get at the people inside. *The Wolves of Willoughby Chase*. Those wolves were vicious. We may have to barricade ourselves in a room." She looked unusually happy at the idea.

Jeremy wrapped his arms around himself and moved away from the windows.

"It's just a story. Wolves wouldn't really do that. They don't like people." Stefan tried to get Raine's attention by nodding his head toward Jeremy, so she would stop saying things to scare the kid, but she wasn't even looking at him.

"What if they're starving?" She pushed on the window again. "I think they'd get over their dislike if they were hungry enough."

Stefan was too tired to reason with her

anymore. "Even if they're starving, they're not traveling through a blizzard to get to us. We could barely move out there, so I'm betting the storm will protect us from ravenous wolves. Okay, now I'm really going to bed. You go ahead and build a fort or whatever it is you want to do."

Chapter 10

SPATTERS

Up in his room, Stefan turned on the television and collapsed on the bed, too exhausted to pull his pajamas out of his suitcase. All the shows on television were fuzzy, and he couldn't understand a word they were saying, so he settled on a soccer match. Sometime later a chattering voice wove through his brain, but he couldn't rouse himself up enough to check it out. He thought about getting up to brush his teeth, and then decided it was too much effort.

The next time he woke, he had a mouthful of wolf fur. Gingerly reaching a hand out, he found the rest of the wolf. Boris licked his face.

"Hey, whose bed do you think this is?"

He heard a low growl from the corner. "Okay, you're here," he said to Boris. "Who's over there? I'm guessing from the growl, it's Natasha." He couldn't see anything. It was dark, completely dark. The television was off. He tried to get his eyes adjusted but they wouldn't cooperate. Stefan had never even imagined such blackness. When the electricity went out at home, there was enough of a glow from outside, but now he could see nothing. He closed his eyes and opened them again. There wasn't any difference between the two. No city lights in the distance and definitely no glow from the moon or any stars.

Before he could decide if he wanted to go back to sleep until the power came back on, Raine screamed and he bolted upright.

"Stefan! Jeremy!" He heard Raine's voice. "Did you hear that terrible screeching?"

"What happened?" Jeremy's sleepy voice called out from the next room over.

"Stay put," Stefan called. "The power is out." He stubbed his toe on a table leg but made it to the door. The hallway was just as dark. A tiny glow came from the doorway of another room.

It was Cecil's pipe and Cecil. "I gather we have lost our electricity," the man said.

"What was that horrible noise?" Raine came out into the hallway wrapped in a blanket.

"I didn't hear anything," Stefan said.

"I heard it," Cecil said. "Rather frightening, somewhat like one imagines a banshee would shriek."

Jeremy came out of his room. "I have my flashlight." He shone it toward Stefan. The light passed over him and then Jeremy screamed. "There are big dark blobs right beside you!"

"It's Boris," Stefan said, "and Natasha, I think. I didn't get a good look at her. They got out of the library. I don't know where Phoebe is."

"I won't ask for a lengthy explanation of why the wolves were inhabiting the library and now are not until we have some more light. Let's get some candles." Cecil held out his lighter. "Stefan, dear boy, could you bring some from the dining room? I do not see well in the dark."

"What about the screeching?" Raine asked, wrapping the blanket more tightly around her.

They all stood still for a moment listening. The lodge was completely silent.

"I didn't hear anything," Jeremy said.

"For the moment, I suggest we worry about light." Cecil took a puff of his pipe. "If we hear the noise again, we'll worry about that then."

"You can take my flashlight, Stefan," Jeremy said, holding it out.

Stefan couldn't see much of anything at first as he moved down the hall, but his eyes were adjusting just a little. Jeremy's tiny flashlight and Cecil's lighter didn't do much good. He fumbled his way down the stairs. It was spooky walking through the deserted lodge. There was only dark nothingness outside the window. Once he had two candles lit, everything looked better. It wasn't a big deal to be without power, he told himself. It happened at least once every winter at home. When he came back into the lobby the others were at the top of the stairs.

"Stefan, if you hold the candles up, we can see enough to come down," Raine said. She led the way, still wrapped in a blanket, looking like a queen leading a procession. The wolves brought up the rear.

When they had all reached the bottom, Stefan handed one of the candles to Cecil.

"I have been briefed on the events of last night," Cecil said, "and I'm rather surprised I slept through it all. So here we are, trapped in an empty hotel in the aftermath of a storm. Rather reminiscent of my favorite movie, but let's hope this particular hotel isn't haunted."

"Haunted?" Jeremy whispered.

"I'm only joking, young one. Sorry, I forget not everyone shares my sense of humor." Cecil looked eerie in the light from the candle, more tired even than the night before. "I know it's not in our contracts to make do in such circumstances, but we shall be troupers. In my early days as part of a traveling theater group, we often had to cope with various disasters. I suppose we shall manage now until rescued." Cecil struck a pose like he was taking a stand against an enemy.

"I'm sure people will be back as soon as it's daylight and they can get across the bridge," Stefan said. He wanted to point out that they hardly needed to be rescued, since they were just standing around in a hotel, but Cecil appeared to be enjoying himself too much.

"What if they can't get across the bridge?" Jeremy asked.

"They'll figure out a way to get here." Stefan didn't want Jeremy to get all worried. "It's not like we really are on an uninhabited planet."

"There aren't any other roads," Raine said. "I have a map with my schoolwork that I was looking at last night. The road here must have been built just for the lodge, because it ends at the parking lot."

"Well, we can't do anything about it, so I'm not going to worry." Stefan yawned. "What time is it?"

"It's only six A.M.," Raine said.

No wonder he was still so tired.

"What should we do?" Jeremy asked.

"We'll just have to hang out until people get back," Stefan said. "I'm going to go get a warmer sweater." Back in his room, he did a quick check under the bed. No Phoebe. It was a little unnerving to think of a wolf roaming around the lodge, but at least it was Phoebe and not Natasha. Phoebe was too timid to do something like leap at him. Natasha he wasn't so sure about.

Pulling his sweater over his head, he headed downstairs to find Raine and Jeremy stuffing the fireplace so full of logs, they had almost completely filled the opening. Cecil sat in one of the big chairs, smoking his pipe and staring off into space. Boris sat beside him. Natasha was over by the door, standing as if expecting to be let out.

"Why are you blocking up the fireplace?" Stefan asked.

"We're not." Raine sat back. "We're going to need to light a blazing fire so we don't get hypothermia and die."

"You're being a little dramatic here, don't you think? The power has only been off a few hours, and we're inside a building. I don't think we need to worry about hypothermia just yet."

"It's better to prepare." Raine's eyes were shining, and she looked excited, like she was on her way to a party. "To survive a disaster, we have to use everything we can."

"Raine, the power is out. That doesn't qualify as a disaster."

"The cell phones aren't working! We tried them."

"So the storm caused a cell tower problem. That can't really be put in the same category as a disaster."

"But the storm is like a disaster. We may have to break up the furniture and burn it to keep warm." Raine moved a lamp off an end table and then dragged the table closer to the fire. She tipped it on one side and started wrenching on one of the legs. "They do this in stories all the time."

"Let's not start with the furniture right away," Stefan said. "There's way too much wood in the fireplace right now. When that burns down, there's probably more outside. You know, in a woodpile, where people keep wood."

"Okay, but if there isn't, I think I can get this leg off." She gave another pull.

Raine's energy and her strange enthusiasms were wearing him out. What he really wanted was to go back to bed, but instead he said, "We'll light the fire, but we need to take some of the logs out." He knelt down and pulled out enough so there was room for some air.

"So you really know how to build a fire?" Raine asked.

"Sure, it's not that hard. Don't you?"

"No, it's not like I was ever a Girl Scout. We have gas fireplaces at home and we just turn on a switch. Is he doing it right, Cecil?"

"Don't ask me, my dear. I know what you are thinking, given my advanced age, but I am not old enough nor of the right nationality to have been a pioneer. And I've never enjoyed rustic holidays where one huddles around a fire." He took a puff on his pipe and blew out a smoke ring. "However, I do believe one simply puts the logs in the fireplace, lights them, and occasionally prods at them with the appropriate implement. My lighter is on the table if you need it."

At first the fire was smoky, but Stefan finally got it to draft, all too aware he had an audience watching his every move.

"Now what?" Jeremy asked.

"I'm going to bring another blanket down here and wait until the power goes back on. I'm already freezing." Raine held out her hand. "My fingers are turning blue. I think I might have frostbite."

"Your fingers would turn white if you had frostbite," Stefan said. "And since it's at least sixty degrees in here, you're not in any danger yet."

"Not yet," she said darkly. "But I am cold. I'm not used to it." She moved over to the fire and held her hands in front of it.

"I wonder when the cook will wake up," Jeremy said. "I'm hungry."

"I don't think the woman is staying here," Cecil said, "though it would be nice if she were. I am in dire need of coffee."

"I'm sure there's plenty of leftover desserts," Stefan said.

"Awesome!" Jeremy said. "Do you think we can just go get some?"

"Why not? The kitchen isn't locked up."

"Yes, I suppose we could raid the kitchen,"

Cecil said. "I am a bit peckish myself."

The kitchen was enormous, with a big fireplace at one end and a huge table in the middle that was bigger than most dining rooms. The space hadn't been fixed up much, except for one restaurant-sized refrigerator. The wolves had followed them in and they began padding around sniffing at things, no doubt looking for food.

Cecil fiddled with the knobs on the stove. "Ah ha! As I hoped, a gas stove, electricity not needed. Jeremy, look in the refrigerator for some milk and I'll try to find some chocolate to melt in it. I shall join you in some hot chocolate."

Stefan went over to a counter along one wall that had several plates covered in foil sitting on it. He was about to uncover one when Raine grabbed his sleeve. She pulled him toward the door, a finger to her lips, so he followed her out into the dining room.

"Did you see them?" she whispered.

"What?"

"Ssshhh!! I don't want Cecil to hear. When you go back in the kitchen, look on the floor. There are drops of blood there! Something terrible happened in the kitchen last night! That's why I heard shrieking!"

Chapter 11

MISSING

"You're imagining things!" Stefan said. "Are you always like this?"

"Like what? Oh, never mind, that's not important. Where did the blood come from? Where *is* the cook?"

"Maybe it isn't blood. Maybe the cook spilled something."

"The kitchen is spotless except for those blotches. Do you think she would spill something and not clean it up?" Raine paced back and forth, scanning the dining-room floor like she was looking for blood spots there, too.

"I don't know." Stefan sighed. "Maybe she got tired and planned to clean it up this morning when she got back."

"Did she ever really leave?" Raine said. "I don't think she did. It was Cecil. I knew I should never have agreed to do this movie. It's cursed and it's all because of Cecil. First the blizzard and then the cook missing and probably murdered. I wonder what he did with her body?"

"Raine, you're crazy! You see some spots on the floor and then you leap to a murdered cook, just because of some silly stories about a curse! You can't really believe that old man killed the woman. Why would he do that?"

"He might be a homicidal maniac."

"That's ridiculous! I want to see this so-called blood."

He pushed open the door to find Cecil, wearing an absurdly small ruffled apron, humming away as he stirred a pot on the stove. The two wolves sat next to him, observing his every move. "Everything all right?" Cecil asked.

"Fine," Stefan said, trying to stroll casually over by the sink, taking quick glances at the floor without being obvious. In the dim light he could make out some dark splotches, but he couldn't really tell what they were. Probably just jam. Raine was too dramatic for her own good. "Jeremy, did you find anything good?" he asked, determined to ignore the crazy girl.

"I found some sort of cake, vanilla I think. Should we eat it?"

"Cake works for me," Stefan said. "People eat coffee cake for breakfast, so why not real cake?" Raine could just eat cold lentil soup if she didn't want too much sugar.

"I'll bring the hot chocolate," Cecil said. "Gather up some plates and forks, will you? I do not eat without utensils."

Boris came over to Stefan and barked at him.

"What about the wolves? They're hungry too." Jeremy opened some drawers until he found the silverware. "What are we going to feed them?"

"After we eat, we can go get them some food from their motor home," Stefan said. "They'll just have to wait a little bit." Raine kept trying to get his attention, but he did his best to pretend he didn't notice. She'd just drag him off again, and he wanted his hot chocolate first.

Cecil led the way back to the main room, putting the tray down on a table near the fire. "This is rather cozy, I must say. Reminds me of my childhood and my dear old gran. Help yourselves."

"Where's Kep?" Jeremy asked, cutting a giant

slice of cake. Boris and Natasha sat down in front of him like they were expecting a piece too.

"Who's Kep?" Cecil asked. "Exactly how many wolves *did* you bring inside?"

Raine had followed them but was keeping her distance from Cecil. "We're calling Mr. Snuggums Kep now," she said coolly.

"Oh," Cecil raised an eyebrow. "Fine choice. I believe Beatrix Potter had a beloved dog named Kep. She made him a character in *The Tale of Jemima Puddle-Duck*."

Raine flushed bright red. "Kep's in his dog bed, I guess. I'd better check on him. Stefan, will you help me?"

"I'd like to eat."

"No! We need to find Kep right now!"

Stefan glanced at Cecil and Jeremy. They didn't seem to notice Raine was acting strangely, but he decided he'd better go with her before she got any stranger.

Upstairs in her room, she shut the door and leaned against it like she expected Cecil to break in. "So did you see the blood?"

"Did you see Cecil in that apron?" Stefan countered. "Does he look like a homicidal maniac?"

"Well, no," Raine admitted, "but the cook is still

missing. And one of the wolves. Maybe the wolf did it. Hunted her down in the night and dragged her off."

Stefan thought his head would explode. "Even though the cook is not a very big person, I don't think Phoebe could drag her away. Besides, wouldn't there be way more blood?" He stopped himself. What was he saying? The cook must be at her own house making some fantastic breakfast for herself, glad the storm gave her an excuse not to go to work.

"I don't know! Something strange is going on."

"I'm not going to argue with you. Will you just see if your dog is here? The hot chocolate is getting cold fast." Not surprisingly, Kep had the most ornate dog bed Stefan had ever seen. It was a fabric gingerbread cottage complete with curtains on the windows and dog-bone–shaped window boxes beneath them.

Raine knelt down to peer inside. "He's not there! Why wouldn't he come looking for me?"

"Maybe he smells the wolves and he's hiding somewhere because he's scared of them. I would be scared, if I were a little dog."

"We have to look for him, and I want to find the cook. Don't you think it's weird Cecil isn't concerned?"

"No, but let's go ahead and find Kep. And when we don't find the body of the cook, will you be satisfied that she just went home? You can't spend all day eyeing Cecil like he's going to pull out a butcher knife at any moment."

"How would the cook get home in the middle of the storm?"

"I don't know. The storm died down sometime in the night. Maybe she had a car with chains on the tires. Maybe someone came and got her with a snowplow on a truck, or on a snowmobile." There had been a chattering voice in the hallway when he had woken up in the night. It had to have been the cook. "It only makes sense that if she's not here, she found a way to get to her house." Stefan hoped Raine would be satisfied with one of those explanations.

"I want to keep looking just to make sure," she said.

It felt odd opening the doors to other people's rooms. Some of them were locked, and Raine asked, "What if the cook's in one of the locked rooms?"

"Then we can't do anything, can we? We've covered all the rooms on this floor." He yawned, deciding he would go back to bed after he ate.

"We should check the top floor and then if she

and Kep aren't up there, we should search the cellars. There's probably a whole network of them under the lodge. We'll need to make torches to explore them." Raine waved her hands around and Stefan could tell she was getting enthused with her own ideas, back to envisioning herself as Nancy Drew creeping through some moldy dungeon.

"I'm not making torches to go into the basement," Stefan said. "I draw the line there. In fact, I'm going back downstairs."

"Fine, I'm sure Jeremy will go into the cellars with me."

"Fine. I'm sure you'll both have fun."

He took a few steps toward the stairs and then Raine said in a soft voice, "Will you please just help me look on the third floor? It will only take a second. I'm really worried about Kep."

Even though he knew she was just using a new tactic to get him to do what she wanted, it was hard to say no. "Okay," he agreed. "A quick look." He should probably look for Phoebe anyway.

As they headed up the third-floor stairs, the smell stopped Stefan halfway. It wasn't the same odor as before. Now it was stronger, rank, and sour, like raw meat doused in vinegar.

"I don't know, Raine." Stefan grabbed her arm before she could go any farther. "Maybe we shouldn't go up there. You smell it, right?"

She faced him, her skin very pale. "I smell it. We have to look. I just need to know. Don't you ever feel like that? When even if something is going to turn out bad, it's better to know it?" Shaking his hand off, she ran up the stairs like she didn't want to give herself a chance to stop.

Stefan followed, but when he turned the corner, Raine was coming back. She ploughed into him like she was trying to get away from something. They teetered at the top of the stairs for a second, and then he reached out to balance himself with the wall. Raine's eyes were wild but she didn't speak. Over the top of her head, Stefan could see the hallway. It was spattered with blood and feathers and pieces of owl, like the bird had exploded. He closed his eyes, trying not to be sick.

"At least . . . at least, it was just an owl," Raine said, her back to the hallway and her eyes fixed on his face. "That was the noise I heard, the screeching sound. That was when it was being killed. I wonder which wolf did it?"

"It doesn't matter," Stefan said. "I'm sure any of them could have." It was a sharp reminder that no matter how much the wolves acted like dogs, they weren't. "They're hunters, and the owl was here to be hunted. Let's go back downstairs."

"No, I have to find Kep. What if he's hiding somewhere because the wolves were trying to get him?"

"Raine, I don't know. Maybe we should wait until some other people get back." He didn't want to tell her what he feared, that they'd find the little dog in the same state as the owl. It would be too awful for her to see, too awful for all of them.

"I have to look for him. You don't need to come with me."

He sighed, knowing he couldn't let her do it herself. "Okay, let's just take a quick look. I can't stand this smell for long." Covering his nose with his sleeve, he followed her as they picked their way down the hall, opening doors as they went. They passed the trainers' room. It still smelled like peanut butter, and Stefan could see little mouse tracks all over the floor, like the mice had wallowed in the peanut butter and been too full to clean their paws.

The last door at the end of the hall was open partway. Stefan slowed down as they approached it. "Let me go first," he said. There was no sound from inside the room, so he pushed the door open gradually. Inside he saw a dark furry shape and almost backed right out.

"What is it?" Raine whispered. She went around him before he could stop her. When Stefan's eyes adjusted he could make out Kep and Phoebe curled up together on an old bearskin rug. Kep lifted his head and gave one little bark, then put it back down on Phoebe's front paw. The wolf licked the smaller dog's head and then laid her chin down on his back. A couple of owl feathers rested on the rug next to them.

"Aren't they cute!" Raine went over and reached down but drew her hand back when Phoebe growled. "I guess I won't pick him up. She's acting like his mother or something."

"Maybe Phoebe thinks he's a mutant wolf cub, and she's adopted him. Or maybe she thinks he's a toy because he wears clothes," Stefan said. Kep had on dog pajamas, a flannel top with teddy bears on it. Phoebe licked Kep's head again, and Stefan realized he couldn't smell the dog perfume any longer.

"I guess she won't hurt him, even if she's the one who ripped the owl apart." Raine glanced back toward the hallway.

"So are you satisfied?" Stefan asked. "The wolf didn't devour Kep. Now can we go have some cake?" His rumbling stomach was at war with itself, the smell from the hallway mixing with the hunger pains.

"But we haven't found the cook. And I know that's blood in the kitchen, no matter what you say. If one of the wolves killed the owl, what else would they kill?"

"Not a person. I keep telling you the cook went home."

"How did she do that? Was her car here?"

"I don't know, but it's the only thing that makes sense. There were a lot of cars in the parking lot."

"I think she's around somewhere. We should search the cellars. And don't leave me alone with Cecil. I can't believe he mentioned *The Shining*. That's the favorite movie he was talking about when he mentioned it took place in an empty hotel after a storm. You can see where his mind is going. We may have to hide the butcher knives and the axes."

Stefan knew that movie. It was the scariest one he'd ever seen. "I don't think Cecil is imagining himself trapped in a hotel in a blizzard, going insane, and trying to murder everyone. For the last time, we are not in a movie, okay? Real life is not like a movie. Just because Cecil made a joke about a movie doesn't mean anything."

"Just remember, if he comes after you with an ax, I warned you," she said.

"Okay," Stefan said, "but please let's at least drink the hot chocolate while it's still warm. And let *me* tell them about the owl."

Downstairs Stefan picked up a mug and took a gulp of it before someone could find a reason to stop him. The warmth and the sweetness of the chocolate were fantastic. He closed his eyes, wishing he could just pretend he was still asleep, about to wake up to other people taking care of things. He took a few more sips and a bite of cake and then another. Hot chocolate and cake might be the best breakfast combination ever.

He was about to take another bite when Raine opened her mouth like she was going to speak. "Wait, Raine," he said, holding up his hand and ignoring the glare she gave him. He filled in Jeremy and Cecil on Phoebe and Kep. When he got to the owl, he tried to keep it as brief as possible, determined to out-talk Raine if she jumped in with any gory details. Jeremy didn't need to know them, and they could keep the kid away from the third floor so he wouldn't find out.

Jeremy made a few sympathy noises about the owl but didn't seem too upset. He put down his plate and petted Boris. "I fed these guys a little cake, but I think they want something. Phoebe and Kep are probably getting as hungry as these two." Stefan looked at Raine, hoping she wouldn't blurt out something about Phoebe being full of owl.

"What do you . . ." Jeremy started to say, but then he stopped and coughed. A distinct wheeze sounded at his next breath.

"Jeremy, if the wolves are making your asthma worse, maybe you shouldn't pet them so much," Cecil said.

"It might not be them; it might just be the cold. Besides, the wheezing is no big deal. I'll go get my inhaler in a minute. Hey, I remembered something good while you were upstairs. There's a woodpile on the side of the lodge by an old shed. Yesterday, while you and Raine were practicing your scene, I went outside to try to find the spot where you'd seen the wolf, and I saw the shed and the wood. I'll show you."

"No, I'll find it. You'd better stay here if the cold makes the asthma worse," Stefan said.

"I'll go too," Raine said. "We can get wolf food and wood. Just wait until I get dressed."

Stefan took advantage of Raine's absence and polished off the rest of the cake, feeling a little more awake after that.

When she came back downstairs and they got outside, Stefan was amazed to see just how much more snow had fallen. Everything on the set was buried under several inches of white. The cleared pathways from the day before were mostly gone and the cold was intense. Stefan's gloves, hat, and jacket didn't do much good.

Raine pulled a map out of her coat. "I've been trying to figure out how people are going to get back here if the bridge is out," she said, opening up the map. "There's another bridge here." She pointed at one spot. "It's only about fifty miles from the village, but after you cross that bridge the road goes in the other direction. Then there's no road that leads here. If they can't get across the village bridge, we're really cut off." She sounded happy at the prospect.

"And that's a good thing? A few minutes ago you were worried about Cecil murdering people."

"Nothing like this has ever happened to me before," she said. "It just seems exciting. And it's so beautiful here," Raine said. "Let's make snow angels!" She flopped down in the snow and almost disappeared from sight. She sat up again. "Wow! I didn't expect it to be so deep. Come on, Stefan!"

"I'm not a snow angel kind of guy," he said, but he had to smile at how happy she was. Being snowbound agreed with her. Now she seemed more like a little kid than a snobby actress. When she got up, she was so covered in snow she looked frosted.

"That's going to make you more cold," he warned. "Maybe even give you hypothermia."

"Really?" she said, her eyes wide.

"No, I'm kidding. You can't get hypothermia from making a snow angel."

"I don't care for once," Raine said. "I'll just warm up in front of the fire when we're done. Let's get the wood first, warm up for a few minutes, and then go back for wolf food."

The shed and the woodpile were on the opposite side of the lodge from the wolves' motor home and the mockup of the spaceship, almost on the back corner of the building by the parking lot. Nobody had shoveled anywhere near the dilapidated structure, so plowing through the snow up to their knees made for slow going. Stefan thought if they were going to haul a bunch of wood inside, they really needed a pathway. Maybe he could find the snowblower one of the crew had been using the day before.

"Here, how many pieces can you carry?" he asked, picking up a log. The wood was so old, some of it crumbled in his hand.

Raine held out her arms. "Just stack them on top of each other."

"Hi!" Jeremy yelled from the back door. "I think the wolves have to go to the bathroom so I'm bringing them outside." Two of the wolves dashed out like crazy animals. Stefan could make out Boris from his size and Natasha from the white patch on her chest. No sign of Phoebe. She probably wouldn't come out until she was desperate. Stefan could see Jeremy holding the door open and making coaxing motions with one hand. Kep zoomed out, jumped off the porch, and vanished into the snow.

"Jeremy, get him! It's too deep!" Raine dropped the logs and took off in a slow-motion run. Jeremy reached down but came up empty-handed as Kep popped up and leaped away. For a little sausage dog he had quite a spring. "Stop!" Raine yelled, picking up her pace. The dog ignored her, barking at Jeremy, who jumped off the porch after him. Figuring Raine and Jeremy would catch Kep eventually, Stefan bent down to gather up the logs Raine had discarded.

Stefan had almost all of the logs in his arms when a distant crack like a gunshot rang out. The sound came from up in the mountains, as if someone were out hunting, though Stefan couldn't imagine who would hunt in heavy snow. He looked toward the others. The wolves were frozen in place. Jeremy had captured the dog and was just handing him to Raine, his arms outstretched, Kep wriggling crazily. Stefan took one step. He heard a rumble, very faint at first. It grew louder, and Stefan thought it was thunder until he glanced toward the mountain.

Chapter 12

WHITE COFFIN

At first Stefan couldn't understand why a billowing cloud of fog hung over just the top of the ski slope. Then the cloud moved and he heard snapping sounds as an immense mass of snow plummeted down the slope, engulfing the trees along the way, breaking them into pieces. They flew up in the air like Pick-Up Sticks and then disappeared back down into the white. The semis and motor homes across the parking lot began to shake.

"Is it an earthquake?" Raine yelled. Stefan realized neither she nor Jeremy could see the mountain of snow coming toward them from where they stood at the back of the lodge. The wolves knew; they lifted their heads and sniffed at the air, then streaked out of sight.

"Run!" Stefan shouted, trying to get his own legs to move. "It's an avalanche!" It was coming right at the lodge. "Cecil!" he yelled.

He saw Cecil's face at one of the back windows and he pointed frantically at the slope and then motioned with his hands. "Get out of the building!" he yelled, though he knew it was hopeless. Cecil wouldn't be able to hear him.

Raine and Jeremy just stood there. "Run!" he screamed again, and then he started toward them, gesturing with his hands at the wolves, hoping someone would understand. Jeremy took a step back toward the building, but then Raine grabbed him and Kep, pulling them after her as she headed down the slope.

When Stefan tried to follow, it felt like he was moving in slow motion through the deep snow. He knew he shouldn't look back, but he couldn't help it. The enormous wave of snow came closer. It was roaring and frothing now, like it was boiling over, a cloud a hundred feet high. The lodge shook violently, and then the snow smashed into it, and Stefan heard cracking and groaning as the building shattered. The windows exploded, bits of glass flying everywhere. Pieces of furniture from the upper stories flew out, and Stefan covered his head with his arms, trying to speed up. The snow was too deep, his legs too tired. He knew he wasn't going to get away. The avalanche was going to catch him and swallow him.

As the cloud came closer Stefan felt a sharp blast of air, like an explosion right at his back, and he lost his balance, tumbling over and over as the snow hit, the force knocking the air out of his lungs. The whiteness came up and swallowed him, and he could feel himself sinking down into it as he fell. He tried to fight, making swimming motions with his arms, except he couldn't tell which way was up. There was snow above and below him and all around him. It filled his mouth and his nose, freezing them, and he clawed at it with one hand, choking for air.

The snow and his body stopped moving, but the relief lasted only an instant. He tried to take a breath but there was no air, and the weight of the snow pressed against him like it was determined to crush him. His hand, now missing a glove, pressed against his mouth and he could just move his fingers, so he reached in and managed to get enough snow out to take a small breath.

His other arm was stuck above his head and he could move those fingers too, but nothing else. As the cold crept through him, Stefan tried to fight the panic, and the coffin of white that was squeezing the life out of him. He wondered how long it would take to die.

Then he heard Raine's voice calling his name, and he wanted to answer her but he couldn't make any sound. He took in one more breath, gagging as the snow went down into his lungs. It made him cough violently and the coughing helped, because the pressure of the snow around him eased a little. He felt a tug on his hand, the one above his head.

"Stefan! Stefan!" It was Raine's voice again and she had a hold on the tip of his glove. "Hold on! I'll dig you out!" Soon he could feel the pressure around his arm loosen a little, and he wiggled it back and forth, wanting to signal he was alive, praying she wouldn't leave him. With his other hand, he made a bigger pocket of air, trying to take shallow breaths so he wouldn't inhale any more snow. When he felt Raine's hand hit the top of his head, a surge of hope ran through him. As soon as she had his face and his hand clear, he brushed frantically at the snow on his mouth, wanting air and light.

As Raine kept digging, he realized he was on his side, under just a few feet of snow, and he knew it was only luck that had saved him. If he had been under two or three more inches of snow she would never have seen his hand. He tried to help, but there was little he could do until she had removed enough of the snow so he could use both his hands. They both dug at his legs, and finally he felt the pressure ease. "You're almost out!" Raine said. Stefan pushed his legs up, breaking free, and then he lay back down, trying to get air in. There was a sharp pain in his side every time he took a deep breath.

Raine's hand touched his face and he looked up at her. Her face was wild, tears streaming down her reddened cheeks. "I saw you go under and I thought you were dead! And then I saw your glove." She broke down, sobbing, and sat down on the ground. He heard a bark and Kep came trotting across the snow toward them.

"Raine, stop crying." Stefan tried to speak up enough so she could hear him over the sobs. "I'm okay. You . . . you saved my life. Don't cry about that."

That only made her cry harder.

"It's all my fault." She rocked herself back and forth, her head on her knees. Kep whined and yipped, trying to get her attention.

"What's your fault? That I'm alive?" He tried to understand, but his head hurt and his side hurt, and he couldn't get rid of the trapped feeling. They needed to get away from here, to somewhere warm and safe so he could understand. They'd get Jeremy and they'd leave, even if they had to walk all the way down the mountain. Then it struck him. Raine was by herself.

"Raine, where's Jeremy?" He tried to reach her face to make her look at him, but she pulled away. If Raine was safe, Jeremy should be safe too. He had seen her grab the kid's arm. "Raine, where's Jeremy?" he repeated.

She kept her head down and her voice was barely audible. "It's all my fault! I thought I was going to drop Kep so I let go of Jeremy."

Stefan forced himself to sit up, even though the pain stabbed at him every time he moved. He found himself looking at a completely changed landscape, unable to get his bearings and confused by the sight of a twisted bed frame a few feet in front of him. He realized he was facing the parking lot; the mounds were the buried motor homes and semis that had been parked there. A few that had been farthest away were just partially buried. What was showing was so damaged, he wondered what was left underneath the snow. When he turned to find the lodge, he wished he hadn't. Only part of one wall was standing. The rest was rubble, like a garbage heap of snow and debris mixed with broken pieces of furniture and glass.

There was no sign of the wolves' trailer or the spaceship. They had been to the front and the side of the ski lodge, right in the main path of the avalanche.

He couldn't see Jeremy anywhere. "Where is he? Why are you just sitting here? Where did you let go of him? We need to try to dig him out!" It was horrible to think of Jeremy slowly suffocating under the snow while they sat and talked.

She lifted her head and pushed the tangled strands of her hair away from her face. "We can't. He . . . he went over the cliff at the end of the parking lot. We almost made it away from the avalanche but then the front edge of it caught us. I didn't stop him."

"What about . . . " Stefan stopped and looked back to where the building should have been.

"Did you see Cecil get out?"

"No," Raine said. "It's just us. The wolves ran away. We're the only ones left."

Stefan struggled to his feet, trying to ignore the pain in his chest. "Are you sure about Jeremy? Maybe he just got covered up with the snow like I did."

"He looked at me when he fell. He was . . . was reaching his hand out for me, and I couldn't catch him. His face was so scared." She bent her head back down to her knees.

"I need to see," Stefan insisted. He wasn't just going to assume Jeremy was dead. Raine pointed but kept her eyes away from his. "It was about right there, near that tree with the top broken off. I don't want to look," she said.

Stefan stumbled over, trying to concentrate on staying on his feet in the mass of debris and snow. From the way the avalanche had come down, he realized he owed his life to the fact that the lodge was slightly to one side of the old ski slope. The central part of the avalanche had hit the lodge on the kitchen side and on the part of the parking lot behind it and extending out from it to the road. Since Raine and Jeremy were behind the lodge, they had had more time to run away when the snow hit; the building had acted like a temporary barrier, even if it had been destroyed in the process. If he hadn't been on the far side of the lodge, just on the edge of the avalanche, Stefan knew he would have been buried under many feet of snow, too many for Raine to find him. The thought of that mountain of snow covering him made him feel sick.

If Raine had escaped, Jeremy should have escaped as well. The very back part of the parking lot on the far side of the lodge was practically clear; the avalanche hadn't reached that far. The skimmers on their trailers were still in place, looking just as they had the night before. Stefan didn't see Jeremy. Part of the stone wall was showing as well, but if Jeremy had been caught by the avalanche, he would have gone over in the area where the snow had pushed over it.

Stefan climbed up on the wall closest to the edge of the avalanche snow, trying to ignore his pain. There were still a few feet of ground between the wall and the rim of the cliff, enough room for the tree Raine had pointed to. It was the one he had noticed the day before, but now all that was left of it was a jagged point where the trunk had snapped and a few of the lower branches. Hoping the roots of the tree were still firmly anchored in the ground, Stefan grabbed it and steadied himself. He didn't know if he really wanted to see over the edge, but if he didn't look for Jeremy, he wouldn't be able to forgive himself. Taking as deep a breath as he could manage, he leaned forward.

Except for jagged pieces of rock jutting out, the cliff face dropped away almost vertically. The sheer drop ended about forty feet down, where the lower part of the mountain met it. He didn't see any signs of Jeremy in the snow at the bottom of the cliff, or off in the distance as the mountain sloped down in the direction of the village.

All the snow was smooth and unbroken. Stefan had never thought he was scared of heights, but the drop-off was so much steeper than he'd realized, it made his head spin. He closed his eyes for a few seconds, waiting for the dizziness to pass. When he opened them, he forced himself to take one more look. Jeremy had to be somewhere.

Stefan shifted over to the other side of the tree. Holding it even tighter in case the dizziness came back, he looked again. Still nothing. He was about to give up when he caught sight of a dark spot against the snow on a small ledge about fifteen feet down the cliff.

"Raine, I see him!" He leaned out as far as he dared. The dark spot was a boot, and it was attached to a leg.

Raine came running. "Where? Let me look!"

"He's really hard to see. I need you to hold on to my arm. No, wait. If I hold on to you, can you lean out and look right down there?" Stefan pointed at the spot below them. "There's a ledge and I see his leg, but I can't see anything else. You aren't scared of heights, are you?" He thought he was strong enough to hold her if she got dizzy, but he didn't really want to test it.

"I'm not scared," she said. "I love things like rock climbing."

"Good." Stefan braced his foot at the base of the uphill side of the tree. He wrapped his left arm around the trunk and held out his right hand for Raine. His left side ached, but the pain eased a bit when he leaned into the tree. It had to be his ribs. He had cracked one years ago falling off a porch roof he shouldn't have been on, and even though the pain was worse now, it was in about the same spot.

Raine took his hand and edged out to the side. Stefan kept his eyes fixed on her feet, ready to pull her back if they showed signs of slipping.

Kep came up and went to the edge like he wanted to see what was below, his paws knocking snow loose. If the dog went over and Raine grabbed for him, Stefan knew he wouldn't be able to hold her. He shouldn't have worried; Kep was actually smarter than he looked. The dog backed off and went to lie down in the snow a few feet back from the edge, panting as if it were the middle of summer.

"I see Jeremy!" Raine cried. "Jeremy, Jeremy! Stefan, if we move this way, we can see him better." Raine picked a spot about three feet away from the tree and then lay down on her stomach. "This is much better."

Stefan lay down next to her and pushed himself out just enough to see over the edge. Down below him Jeremy was on his hands and knees crawling along the ledge. "Jeremy! Are you okay?"

The boy looked up. "What happened?" he asked, a confused look on his face, as if he had just woken up from a deep sleep. Stefan was horrified to see the snow right next to Jeremy fall away down the cliff, leaving one of the boy's feet sticking out in the air.

Chapter 13

THE CLIFF

"Stay still! Don't move!" Stefan screamed, panicked, looking around for a way to get down to the kid. He couldn't find one. Jeremy seemed dazed, but he stopped moving. Stefan tried to talk fast so he would understand. "You're on a ledge on the side of the cliff. I don't know how much of it is snow, and how much is rock. Can you crawl closer to the face of the cliff?"

Stefan held his breath while Jeremy inched away from the edge. More snow tumbled away with every motion the boy made. When he stopped, they could see only the soles of his boots. The rest of him was blocked from view by an overhang, another section of the cliff that jutted out a few feet below them. Jeremy didn't make a sound, and Stefan realized there was no sound anywhere. It was as if they really were on an uninhabited planet, the snow erasing any hint they'd even been there.

"Jeremy, say something!" Stefan called.

The boots disappeared and then they saw Jeremy's head on the other side of the jagged edge. "I'm standing up," he said. "The ledge isn't very wide but it feels sturdy. What should I do?" Stefan had no idea.

"Jeremy," Raine called, "I'm sorry I let go of you. Are you okay?"

There was silence and then a small voice said, "Yes. Don't talk to me. Stefan, are you still there? What should I do?"

"Stay still until we figure something out. Raine, try your cell phone. Maybe they can get a helicopter up here."

"I don't have my cell phone," she said. "I laid it down in my room when I went to get dressed and I didn't put in back in my pocket, because I knew I needed to charge it if the power went back on."

"Jeremy, do you have yours?" Stefan looked back over the edge. From where he stood, he could see Jeremy clearly.

"No, I just put my coat on over my pajamas. I was going to get dressed once the wolves came back inside. I'm cold."

Stefan wished there was some way to know if anyone was even trying to get to them yet. It seemed like days had passed since they had first woken up, but when he added up the events, he knew it could only be a few hours. People down in the village were probably either still sleeping or just sitting around drinking coffee, waiting for the snow to stop, having no real reason to worry about getting back to the lodge right away. Knowing Heather, his aunt wouldn't even be awake yet. With the bridge closed, even when they did start to worry, what could they do? Unless he and Raine did something soon, Jeremy would either freeze to death or fall off before anyone came back.

"One of us should try to go for help," Stefan said. "I know I saw some houses on this side of the bridge close to the village when we drove up here. We could climb down and walk to one of them."

He looked at Raine. She had gotten up and was just standing there looking off in the distance, holding on to her dog.

"Raine, did you hear me? One of us needs to go for help."

"How?" she said, pointing. "Didn't you see what happened to the road?"

Stefan moved closer to her and saw what she had been staring at. The road came up to the bottom of the cliff and then disappeared under the snow. The avalanche had filled in the section of the mountain that had been cut away for access to the lodge. It was now filled with snow, so many feet of snow, it would take heavy equipment to clear it.

"Do you think we can climb down that?" Raine asked.

To Stefan's eyes it looked too steep. "No," he said. "Once we were on it, we might trigger a snowslide and that could turn into a smaller avalanche. I don't want to take the chance." He couldn't stand the thought. There was no other way off the set except straight down the cliff or over the top of the mountains that rose around the plateau where the lodge sat. It would take forever to climb up over the mountains, and there was no way to know if there would be anyone on the other side. They'd have to try something else.

"We need to find some rope," he said. "We'll

have to try to pull him up with it."

"I don't blame him for not wanting to talk to me," Raine said. "I wouldn't want to talk to me either."

"He'll talk to you once you help him back up. Let's just get him off that ledge."

She hugged Kep closer to her. "This is terrible."

"I know, but let's make it not so terrible. It's better to do something besides just sitting here. Come on. We'll be warmer if we're moving too."

"You're right," she said. "Where do we find rope?"

"There was probably rope or cable in some of the semitrailers, if we can get at one that's not completely buried." He had no idea what had been in most of them, because he just hadn't had time to get familiar with everything on set. Still, with the amount of cables and cords the crew kept laying out for the setup of the shots and then rolling back up, they had to have a place to keep it.

"I can do that!" Raine set Kep down and took off toward them. The dog looked after her but didn't follow. He looked at Stefan and whined.

"I'm not picking you up," Stefan said. "Sorry." The dog lay down.

"What's happening?" Jeremy called.

"Just hold on. We're getting some rope to pull you up."

"I'm really, really cold."

"We'll hurry."

Before he could get to the trailers, Raine was already climbing out of one. "This is a camera storage trailer," she said. "It's a total mess in there, and I didn't find any regular rope, but there are cables and cords everywhere." She held out two bright orange extension cords. "Would something like these work?"

Stefan took one from her. It was a heavy-duty outdoor cord wrapped in a coil, so it was thick and strong. Jeremy didn't weigh very much. "It should," he said, "We can try make a harness out of this one like rock climbers use, and then we'll tie the other one on to pull him up." He carried the cord back over to the edge, thinking about what size loops he needed based on the size of the kid, and trying to remember which kind of knot would hold best. He tried square knots, and then doubled them, hoping they'd be good enough. When he was satisfied with the harness, he held it out to Raine.

"What do you think?"

She frowned. "I don't know. Do you think it's

going to hold? I think you should lower me down so I can help him if it starts to come loose, and then you can pull me back up."

"No way. My ribs feel awful, like they're cracked or broken. I don't think I could even get Jeremy up without you."

"Maybe we should think of something different," Raine said.

Stefan didn't know what that something different would be. They didn't have any rescue equipment, and bits of wood and stone weren't going to do them any good. "We need to try this first, okay? Let's fasten your cord to the front of the harness so we have something to pull with." She still looked doubtful, but she did tie the two together. Stefan pulled on the knot when she was done and decided it was secure.

Raine called down, "Jeremy, we're sending a harness down. Just step into it. Put one leg through each opening."

They fed it out until they heard Jeremy yell, "I've got it."

Stefan went back to the edge and knelt down so he could see Jeremy. He held his breath as he watched the boy struggle to get into the harness.

When he had it on, Stefan called, "Ready?"

"Ready!" Jeremy yelled.

Stefan tossed the cord over the lowest, thickest branch of the tree, then grabbed the end. "We'll use the branch to help us," he said. "Like a pulley. You're going to stand in front of me. We'll both pull when I say go." She nodded her head and moved into position. Stefan braced himself and said, "Ready, Go!"

Jeremy started screaming the instant they starting pulling. "No! No! Stop! Stop!"

They couldn't see him from where they stood, so Stefan stopped pulling and yelled, "Jeremy, is the harness holding?"

"Yes, but I'm scraping against the rocks! It hurts!"

Stefan didn't know what to do, but then Raine called, "We'll go slow! Use your hands and your feet to push away from the rocks! We're going to start pulling again."

When there was no answer, they resumed, inching the rope up. It was nerve-racking not being able to see Jeremy. If Stefan hadn't felt the weight, he wouldn't have known the boy was there.

All of a sudden Jeremy screamed. "Ow! Ow! Stop! Stop!"

Raine faltered and Stefan barked, "Keep pulling! He's just in panic mode. We can't stop." He knew if they stopped, they'd never find a way to get Jeremy up, and the kid couldn't stay on the ledge. As they pulled Stefan realized the snow had begun to fall again. It was quickly building up on his face. He couldn't let go of the cord to brush it away, and the snow felt like it was already covering him up. He tried to shake his head to get it off, but the flakes just kept coming. His heart started to race, and he could feel sweat breaking out on his forehead. It was going to bury him.

"I see him!" Raine's voice sounded very far away, and Stefan shook his head again. The dizziness was back. He thought he heard Jeremy crying and Kep barking, but his heart was pounding so hard he wasn't sure. Stefan tried to concentrate on what they were doing, not on the snow he could feel coating his eyes. He had to get the snow off his face, so he took one hand off the cord, just as Raine let go, saying over her shoulder, "Hold tight while I help him up."

His one hand wasn't enough to hold Jeremy's weight and the boy slipped back.

"What are you doing?" Raine yelled. Jeremy screamed and Stefan saw him clawing at the snow on the cliff edge. Raine tried to grab hold of the boy and managed to get hold of the harness, but the weight of him pulled her forward, and her feet slipped out from under her. Without thinking, Stefan took hold of the trunk of the tree with one hand as he lunged forward, taking hold of part of the sleeve on Raine's jacket, pulling her as hard as he could back toward him, hoping she would hold on to Jeremy. He heard screaming and realized he was the one doing it, the pain in his side so extreme it was as if someone had stabbed him. They all fell in a heap next to the tree, gasping for breath. Stefan rolled on his back. He lay still, looking up at the sky, the snowflakes still falling, covering his face, melting into tears.

Jeremy sat up and looked around. "Where's Cecil?" he said.

Chapter 14

BURIED

Stefan didn't have the strength to answer. He didn't want to move or talk until someone came to get them. It would have been nice just hanging out, doing nothing, if he hadn't been so cold. He tried to imagine he was in a park in the summertime, flat on his back in warm green grass, soaking up hot sun. He closed his eyes and then opened them again, blinking away the snowflakes. The cold was too hard to ignore as it seeped into his back and his legs, and the snow just kept falling. Kep came over and acted like he was going to jump on Stefan's stomach, but Stefan pushed him away. Being used as a dog perch wouldn't help his ribs any.

"Isn't anybody going to answer?" Jeremy said. "Where's Cecil?"

"Cecil was in the building," Raine said. "He didn't get out." She grabbed Kep and buried her face in his fur.

"Did you try to find him? Phoebe was inside too. Did you just leave them there?" Jeremy was almost shouting, glaring at Raine.

Stefan looked over at her. She looked like she might cry again. "Jeremy," Stefan said. "The whole building fell down, a three-story building. I . . . I don't think we are going to find them. Not by ourselves. It's been too long anyway. He wouldn't have enough air to survive."

"Did you even look?"

"We haven't had time," Stefan said. "Raine dug me out of the avalanche, Jeremy. I was buried. She saved my life, and then we went looking for you."

"They show people on television being saved from buildings all the time, sometimes days later. We have to look. He's one of us."

Stefan was trying to frame some words to make Jeremy understand when Raine said, "It's the wolves . . . they're back!" Boris padded up and put his nose to Stefan's face. Stefan sat up and ruffled the wolf's fur, a rush of relief racing through him. Having the wolves back made it seem like they weren't so alone. He looked around and spotted Natasha about a hundred feet away, watching them with a wary look on her face, exactly as if she were a wild wolf unused to people.

"Maybe Boris and Natasha can help us look for Cecil and Phoebe. Like rescue dogs!" Jeremy brightened up.

"They aren't trained to do that," Raine said. "And I doubt if they really care about Cecil."

"Maybe they'll at least be able to find Phoebe, since she's part of their pack. I'm going to go try to find him, even if you won't." Jeremy stumbled away from them, falling down and picking himself up again. He looked really small and young in his Spider-Man pajama pants, no older than Stefan's little brother.

"Come on," Raine said. "Let's go help him look, so we can convince him to stop. I don't want him to stay mad at me."

Stefan groaned and made himself get up. "Then we need to figure out how to get warm."

Raine shivered, holding Kep close to her. "I don't know if I'll ever be warm again."

The closer they got to where the building had

stood, the more disoriented Stefan became. The avalanche hadn't hit the lodge straight on but slightly to one side, so the chimney and part of wall on the other side still stood, even though the roof was gone. The side with the kitchen and the dining room was completely destroyed and mostly under a huge mound of snow. Boris ran around sniffing everything. Natasha had moved closer but she was still keeping her distance.

"Cecil!" Jeremy yelled. "Cecil, are you there?"

Stefan wasn't surprised there was no answer, but Jeremy didn't seem discouraged. "We need to dig!" the boy said. "I saw some of the crew putting the shovels away yesterday in a shed. If we can figure out where it was, we might be able to find them."

Stefan didn't want to dig for Cecil, because he knew they would just find the old man's body, and the thought of that made him feel sick. "I'll help," Raine said, putting Kep down. "Tell me where the shed was in relation to the building and I'll try to find it."

"Okay," Jeremy said. "It was over by the props trailer, about right there." The two of them moved away, but Stefan didn't follow. He knew Raine was just making a peace offering to Jeremy.

Surely she didn't think they would find the old man alive.

Where would Cecil have been when the avalanche hit? Stefan had seen him at one of the back windows of the dining room that looked over the parking lot, and then once the building started shaking, wouldn't Cecil have moved to the closest door, the back door? If that part was under many feet of snow, it might convince Jeremy and Raine of the futility in digging.

Stefan used the remaining wall of the lodge to orient himself, trying to visualize the building in his head, so he could find where the back door would have been. There were wooden shingles everywhere, and that made it difficult to figure out what was underneath them. When the avalanche had blown through the building, sections of the roof had come off whole, making it even more confusing.

The snow crunched beneath his feet as he walked back and forth. He shuddered, thinking of the weight pressing against him when he had been underneath it. There was no way Cecil would still be breathing buried beneath it.

His feet were so numb Stefan could barely feel them. Even though it had finally stopped snowing, it was bitterly cold. They really needed to figure out a way to build a fire, or get warm, because he couldn't concentrate when he was so cold. Boris caught his attention. The wolf was pacing around in a tight circle, his nose a fraction of an inch above the snow about where the middle of the lodge would have been. He whined, and Stefan walked over to him. The wolf had stopped at one spot between two roof sections. He whined again.

"Cecil?" Stefan said, the word coming out in a croak. His throat was so dry he didn't know if he could get any louder. The cold air was making his mouth feel like a frozen desert.

Jeremy and Raine came up behind him. "What's happening?" Raine asked. "Did you find something? We didn't find any shovels, but we thought we could use these boards." He saw they were both carrying what looked like some of the wide floorboards that had been on the upper floors of the lodge.

"I think Boris found something." The wolf was now crouched down on the ground, his nose touching the snow. Kep came over to him and sat down, sniffing the air.

"Cecil!" Jeremy yelled. Raine joined in. "Cecil!" they both screamed.

"Wait!" Stefan held up his hand. "I think I hear something. Everybody be quiet." He heard a sound, a very faint but steady tapping noise.

"It's him!" Jeremy started digging frantically. "We'll get you out, Cecil!"

Raine handed Stefan a board, and they all began to dig. The snow was as heavy as wet cement, and it was slow going. Stefan wished he could shovel one-handed, so his side wouldn't hurt so much, but he quickly discovered that was impossible if he wanted to move more than a fraction of the snow at a time.

"Boris, help!" Jeremy motioned to the wolf, who stood watching the three of them. The boy made digging motions with his hands and the wolf cocked his head but didn't join in.

They dug down a few feet and then Stefan held up his hand again. "Stop. Cecil, are you down there?" The tapping increased in both speed and sound, and then they heard a muffled bark.

"It's Phoebe!" Jeremy called. At the sound of the bark, Boris joined in the digging and the wolf made more progress than the rest of them, the snow flying up from his paws in a spray of white.

Stefan's board clunked against something solid. "It's stone, probably part of the foundation," he said. He pushed the board down around it, try-ing to figure out how big it was, trying to find an edge. The board hit something solid again and then he heard Cecil's voice.

"You're right above us! We're under one of the dining room tables." The sound of tapping moved a little to the left. "Here's the edge of the table," Cecil said. "Can you dig here?"

Stefan and Raine positioned themselves on either side so they could take turns shoveling.

"Stop!" Cecil yelled. "I can see some light but the snow is collapsing in, and I don't have much room to get away from it."

Stefan knelt down. He could see a dark hole to one side, so he reached his hand down and pulled out chunks of snow. Phoebe's nose poked through, startling him, and he moved his hand away as she tried to shove her whole head out. Her eyes were crazy with fear.

"It's okay, girl," Stefan said. Boris nearly knocked him over, licking at Phoebe's face. Kep joined in, yipping wildly. Phoebe couldn't get her shoulders out, but she wouldn't quit struggling, her front claws scrabbling at the snow. "Phoebe, no." Stefan put his hand on the top of her head, trying to slow her down. "Cecil, can you call her back?"

"I doubt she's going to listen to me and I can't get hold of her collar. I don't fancy trying to grab her by the tail."

Stefan pulled away more chunks, trying to work around the wriggling wolf. When he had cleared enough away for her to get her shoulders out, he saw a gash along her neck, the blood still trickling out, staining the snow red where she rubbed against it. Phoebe pulled back and then burst out of the opening. She galloped around in a circle, stopping to shake herself off as if she were wet. The cut on her neck was several inches long, the fur around it matted with dark, dried blood. Even though it looked awful, Stefan thought since it wasn't bleeding much now, it couldn't be that serious a wound. The two wolves ran over to Natasha, who seemed to have established a set distance from them that she was not willing to change. Stefan wasn't going to worry about her.

The next step was to get Cecil out. Stefan stuck his head in the opening. "Cecil, can you get over here? I think the opening is big enough for you to climb out."

"I'm afraid I've injured my hip, Stefan. I don't know if I can move well."

Stefan felt Raine's hand on his shoulder. "I'll climb in and help."

Once she was in, Stefan could hear talking, but he couldn't make out what they were saying. Raine reappeared. "He's hurt, but he can crawl over here. We're going to need to get the opening a lot wider because I think it's going to take both of us to help him out."

It took several more minutes to get the opening big enough, either because the chunks of snow were turning to stone, or Stefan was running out of energy. Raine didn't look the least bit tired. She almost dove back into the hole, popping her head up again seconds later with Cecil beside her. Stefan was shocked by the grayness of the man's face. He didn't know anyone could turn that color.

Cecil coughed and ran his hand over his face. "I'm afraid I'm not feeling strong enough to be much help getting myself out. I do apologize."

"Let me get one of my arms under yours." Stefan shifted to one side of the opening. "Raine, you're going to have to get to Cecil's other side so I can use my right arm. My left side is pretty much useless at this point." Between the two of them they managed to pull Cecil out, but it exhausted all of them. Even though Stefan was surprised by how light the old man was, Cecil didn't seem to have any strength in his legs at all to help himself.

They eased him down on the remains of a dresser tipped on its side.

Putting his hand to his chest, Cecil said, "Lesson learned. An avalanche is not good for the old ticker. I can't thank you enough, children."

"How did you end up under a table?" Jeremy asked.

"When I heard the noise and the windows started rattling I ran for the back door but only made it as far as the end of the dining room, where I tripped over Phoebe. I think that saved my life. I didn't see her crouching there. When I heard the whole building creaking, I thought I'd be safer under a table so I crawled under the closest one. Phoebe joined me. Poor creature, she was shaking as much as the building."

Now that they had stopped moving, Stefan could feel the cold again. At least rescuing people kept the cold away, but now that they were done, the cold was the new enemy. Stefan's feet hadn't warmed up much at all, even with the effort to get Cecil out. "Cecil, do you have a cell phone?"

"I don't even own one of them," Cecil said. "I survived seventy years without one and never felt the need to change, though I may now reconsider."

"Somebody will be here soon," Jeremy said. "They aren't going to leave us here for long now that there's been an avalanche."

"How is anybody going to know?" Raine's voice was shaky. "They're all miles away. Nobody but us knows there's been an avalanche. They all think we're just sitting out a storm inside the lodge with our own personal chef and plenty of food. And even once they start to worry we might be in trouble, with the bridge out and the avalanche blocking the road, they can't get to us very fast. We're stuck."

No one said anything, until a wolf's howl, far in the distance, broke the silence.

Chapter 15

WOLF PACK

Boris and the other wolves answered with their own howls, and then the one faraway wolf voice turned into many, how many Stefan couldn't tell. The howls all blended together into one fierce chorus. And their own wolves responded, their muzzles raised to the sky. The sound gave Stefan chills and raised the hair on his arms. The movie animals suddenly seemed much wilder, no longer resembling tame pets.

Raine grabbed Jeremy's arm and pulled him in closer to Stefan and Cecil. "Where are they?" she asked. "I can't tell." The howling echoed around them like it was bouncing off the cliffs.

"Wherever they are, they won't bother us,"

Stefan said with more assurance than he felt. He hoped Hans was right about wolves avoiding humans. The cold was enough of a problem. Boris and the others stopped howling but began to pace back and forth, lifting their noses to sniff the air.

"I thought there was just one wolf," Jeremy said, wrapping his arms around himself.

"They live in packs, so even if Stefan saw just one yesterday, there are probably a lot more," Raine said.

"Why are they howling? Why are our wolves howling back? If they come after us, we don't have any place to hide." Jeremy darted to where they had pulled Cecil out from the avalanche. "Cecil, will we all fit in there? We can hide." He knelt down like he was going to climb in.

"Take it easy, Jeremy," Stefan said. "They aren't even close to us." At that moment, Kep decided to join in, his howls resembling the squeaks of a badly played clarinet. It was so ridiculous, Stefan felt himself smiling.

Cecil chuckled and then coughed. "We shall be fine with such a brave pug to protect us."

Jeremy ran back to them. "I don't want to stay here!"

"We know people will get to us eventually," Stefan said. "We need to concentrate on getting all of us warm and keeping us that way."

"I'm really cold," Raine said. "We should build a fire while we're waiting. Cecil, do you still have your lighter?"

"I do. I used it to light my dungeon briefly." Cecil flexed his fingers. His hands didn't look like they were responding to his brain, and Stefan realized they were probably frozen. Cecil didn't have any gloves on and he wasn't wearing a coat. Even though the man spoke like he was fine, the strange color of his face couldn't be good. What had Cecil meant when he had put his hand to his chest? Did he have heart problems? Stefan pushed that thought away. There was no way they could deal with that.

It took Cecil a few seconds to get his hand in his pocket to draw out the lighter. "Here it is. It would be a happy day indeed if I still had my pipe as well, but I'm afraid it is no more."

"Good . . . I mean about the lighter, not the pipe," Stefan said. "Let's pile some wood up and get a fire going. We'll all feel better. Raine, now you can break up the furniture if you want."

This got a small smile from her, and she ran

over to get a chair already broken in half. There were so many pieces of broken furniture and flooring strewn around, it didn't take long to collect enough debris to make a bonfire.

"Can I light it?" Raine begged. Cecil handed over his lighter and Stefan stood back as she grabbed it, flicking it on the ends of the splintered wood. One bit finally caught, and when it was burning strongly, she used the piece to light the others.

"Isn't this great!" Raine said, grabbing Jeremy by the hands and dancing him around like they were celebrating a victory. The fire didn't exactly blaze and Stefan knew the melting snow underneath the wood would eventually kill the flames, but he didn't want to put a damper on their excitement.

Stefan found two almost whole chairs and carried them close to the fire, then helped Cecil over. After Cecil sat down, Stefan dropped into the chair next to him, feeling like he was about as old as the elderly actor. He didn't know how Raine and Jeremy had the energy to move.

The warmth of the fire was amazing at first, and Stefan felt himself relaxing a little as his toes and his fingers came back to life. Even though he wasn't really afraid of the wild wolves, it was nice to have the flames to keep them away. He knew no wild animal liked fire. Their own wolves were leery of it too. Kep, Boris, and Phoebe had all backed away and were sitting close to each other. He didn't see Natasha at all.

The blaze was really going for the moment. A table leg that had been carved into the shape of an animal's foot caught and glowed like a torch, either the varnish or furniture polish on it crackling and sparking blue.

"We should hold fast to these chairs or dear little Raine will rip them out from under us to burn," Cecil said. "The girl is quite enthralled with flames." Raine smiled in their direction as she threw a few shingles on. Stefan was glad to hear Cecil's voice sounding a little stronger. The man shifted his chair closer to the fire. "I'm glad she appears undaunted by our ordeal. You, however, seem somewhat battered by this unfortunate experience, and you're clearly favoring your left side. What happened?"

"I think I cracked a rib when I fell." Stefan didn't want to explain about the avalanche, about being buried. He didn't look at Cecil; he just kept staring into the fire.

"If I may give advice, you should find something soft to pad that side and then tape the padding on; it will feel better. I suffered a similar injury in my younger days, falling from a balcony during a battle with a werewolf on the set of *Wolfman Fangdango*. Did you ever see that one?"

"No, sorry," Stefan said, wondering where he could find some tape. It would be nice to be wearing dry clothes as well. His jeans were so caked with snow, they were like boards, stiff and frozen. As soon as the fire thawed them, they'd be soaking wet.

"Some thought that movie was a classic," Cecil said, "even though the werewolf costumes were on the low-budget side; big clumps of fur fell off every time the actor sneezed."

"Costumes." Stefan stood up. "Maybe we can get at the costumes to put on, or at least find something to wrap around us." He needed another glove too; his one hand was freezing.

"Sorry?" Cecil said. "I didn't follow."

"Raine!" Stefan called. "We need to get some of the costumes to use as dry clothes. With all this snow falling, we're never going to dry out like this."

"The costumes were inside the lodge," she said, twirling Jeremy around.

"Not the ones with the special effects sewn in," Stefan said. "There were some in the prop trailers. Remember, Cecil?"

"I do, but from what I can see, the trailers didn't fare very well in this event. I don't know where or if we will find the right ones."

"Those trailers were near the end of the row, farther away from the avalanche. Remember Alan told us the monster costumes were in the other trailer, so that means there were two of them. Maybe we can get to at least one. I'm going to look."

"I'll come with you," Jeremy said. "I'm getting cold again."

"Call me if you need any help." Raine dragged over what looked like another floorboard. "The fire's dying down some, so I'll keep it going." She tossed the wood on.

"Guard my chair, Cecil, so Raine doesn't throw it on the fire," Stefan said, and the old man smiled and put one hand on the arm of it.

Since Raine had already been in the camera storage trailer, Stefan and Jeremy headed to one that was tipped over and twisted so that a wall was peeled open, like someone had taken a can opener to it.

Jeremy ran ahead, then started backing up like

he was scared. "Stefan, there's an awful noise in there!" When Stefan reached the trailer, he could hear the sound, a buzzing noise he recognized.

"It's one of the ice spiders," he said. "This is the prop trailer." Inside he took a step and his foot almost slipped out from under him. A container of nails and screws had spilled, carpeting the side of the trailer that was now the floor. The place was full of plastic and metal bins, some thrown open, others just tipped over. A strong chemical smell stung Stefan's nose and made his eyes water, but he couldn't identify it.

The buzzing sound came from one corner, and when Stefan drew close he could see a pile of ice spiders. One had somehow gotten switched on and was circling a small clear area, the legs on one side so smashed they weren't functioning. Its sound card was damaged as well, because the buzzing noise sounded like an ordinary wasp. He picked the spider up and shut it off, dropping it back with the rest of them.

"There's some weird fabric over here," Jeremy said.

Stefan stepped over a tangle of wires to a table that had crashed over.

"There." Jeremy pointed to a bit of fabric

showing from underneath one corner of the table.

"Help me lift it off," Stefan said. They heaved it to one side, uncovering a pile of what looked like wrinkled walrus skin, just as Alan had described. When Stefan reached down to pick one up, it unfolded and he nearly dropped it. Attached to the skin was a hideous baboon-like head that had a gigantic mouth full of long, sharp teeth. It was more frightening than any real animal Stefan had ever seen. If he ever got the chance to finish the movie, it would be easy to pretend to be terrified of these.

"Whoa! Those are really creepy!" Jeremy said.

"I guess if you start with two ugly creatures and morph them together, you'll end up with something even uglier." Stefan examined the fabric part of the costume, trying to avoid looking at the teeth and the glittering black eyes. There were only four costumes, but when they were unfastened in the back, the main body part was about the size of an afghan. "At least they'll make good blankets. We'll just have to ignore the heads. Let's get these to Cecil. Without a coat, he must be freezing even by the fire."

Stefan took three and gave the other to Jeremy to carry. As they made their way back to Cecil,

Stefan spotted Raine up the slope using a small board as a shovel. When she saw them, she yelled, "I've almost uncovered a cooler. Maybe it will have something to eat or drink in it. Throw some more wood on the fire, would you?"

The fire blazed so high, Cecil sitting in his chair was dwarfed by it. He raised his eyebrows at the sight of the monster heads but didn't say anything as they wrapped the costume skins around him, arranging them so the heads were resting on the ground around him.

"They aren't pretty, Cecil, but they'll keep you warm." The old actor nodded, not speaking. He still had the gray look to his face. Stefan didn't know what to do. "Raine," he yelled. "Have you found anything?"

"I've almost got it uncovered!"

"Well, if you find some water, bring some to Cecil, okay?" He knew they could eat snow if Raine couldn't find any water, but after everything that had happened, he didn't want to think about filling up his mouth with snow again.

Cecil smiled up at him, but Stefan wasn't convinced it was a real smile. "We're going to keep looking for some warm clothes, okay?" Stefan said. "That will make you feel better, right?"

Cecil nodded and again waved at them to go.

Boris and Phoebe dashed by, like they had gotten over their concern with the fire, chasing each other around as if they were on some terrific vacation. Running across the snow didn't bother them. Stefan had never noticed until now how big their feet were. It was as if they had their own built-in snowshoes. It would be hard to win a race with a wolf. Kep came over and sat by Cecil's feet, and Stefan noticed the little dog was trembling. Maybe the dog sweaters weren't such a dumb idea.

Jeremy had noticed too. "Cecil, will you hold Raine's dog while we look for some costumes for us? He looks cold." The boy picked up the pug and when Cecil mouthed a "yes," he put the dog in his lap.

"Let's try that other trailer," Stefan said, pointing past the one they had just explored to one that was only partially buried, tilted on its side, and held at the angle by the snow surrounding it. "The prop trailers were probably right next to each other, so we may be in luck."

When they reached it, Stefan thought it looked too crushed for them to find a way in, but Jeremy climbed around and called out, "There's an opening here. I think I can squeeze in." Stefan pulled himself up on the top of the trailer beside the boy. One of the ventilation panels had cracked and opened slightly before the snow piled up around it.

"It's dark in there though, really dark," Jeremy said.

"You don't happen to still have your flashlight, do you?"

"No, I left it in the lodge."

"Go get Cecil's lighter then. That should help. Let me see if I can make a bigger opening." Stefan pulled at the panel, trying to wrench it open. He couldn't move it more than a few inches. It was still too small for him to get in. The kid would fit and possibly Raine, but he didn't even want to try.

When Jeremy came back waving the lighter, he asked, "Does Cecil have asthma too? He's breathing like he does."

"I don't know," Stefan said. "He was trapped for a long time. He might just be out of breath from that. He'll probably feel better once he rests."

"I hope so." Jeremy handed Stefan the lighter. "I don't know how to work this."

Stefan showed him and then pulled on the panel until he thought it was wide enough for

Jeremy. "If it's the prop trailer, there should be some of the costumes like we were wearing yesterday in there. Bring as many as you can find, because we can put them on in layers."

Jeremy disappeared inside, and Stefan heard metal things banging together. "Are you okay?" Stefan called.

"Wow, there's a lot of junk in here!" Jeremy's voice sounded from inside the trailer.

Stefan shifted so he wouldn't block what little light there was. "Do you think you're in the right trailer?"

"How am I supposed to know?"

"Just look for costumes or anything else we can use to keep warm."

"There's a metal box and it's full of tubes labeled "pyrotechnics." I bet they're the fireworks for that scene where the spaceship blows up!"

"Jeremy, get the lighter away from those!"

"Oh, right, I forgot! There must be a hundred tubes in here!"

"They're not going to keep us warm, Jeremy. Would you keep looking?" Stefan hoped Jeremy didn't trip with the lighter in his hand. They didn't need an exploding trailer on top of everything else.

"I'm looking! There's some gooey stuff spilled on the floor though. I don't want to step in it."

Probably alien intestines. That wouldn't do them any good either.

"It smells funny in here . . . I think I found them. No, wait. It's the inflatable mattresses the stuntmen use for falls. We could use those as blankets too."

"Maybe, if we need them. Keep looking for the costumes. That's what we need most."

"I feel something soft. Here they are."

Jeremy pushed costumes, both tunics and pants, one after the other out through the opening. "There's only five that I can see."

"Try to find those sweater shirts that go underneath the tunics." Stefan wanted as many layers as possible.

He heard a crunching sound on the snow and turned to find Raine coming toward him, holding out a roll of black tape.

"Cecil told me about taping your ribs and I remembered seeing the gaffer tape in the camera trailer when I climbed in to get the cords. Will it work for them?" She held it out.

"I don't know, I've never used it, but I'm willing to try anything." It looked like black duct tape, but when she gave it to him, he could feel the tape was more like cloth. As long as it stuck to him, he didn't really care what it was made of.

Jeremy's head poked out of the opening. He had streaks of blue on his face. "This is fun, like a treasure hunt!"

"What's on your face?"

"Paint. Some spilled and I put my hand down in it accidentally." He handed out a stack of costume shirts, then a tattered plaid flannel shirt. "What about this? It's really big and it has some rips in it."

Stefan took it. The shirt smelled like varnish. "It must be Alan's," he said. "I'll take it for my ribs." He folded it into a square, tempted just to wrap his nearly numb hand in the softness of it. "Jeremy, look for gloves too, okay? I'm going to go change in the other prop trailer. Raine, will you stay here and help Jeremy?"

The other trailer had one small section still blocked on three sides from the wind, so Stefan climbed over some of the equipment to find a clear place to change. He managed to get the pants on, but when it came time to tape his ribs, he fumbled with the whole process. It was almost impossible to hold the padding and tape one-handed. He was also freezing without a shirt on, like he had plunged into an ice-cold lake. The tape kept sticking to his fingers and getting tangled up.

Raine's voice called from the other side of the trailer. "You're taking a long time! Jeremy's putting on his costume in the other trailer and I want to change too."

"I'm still taping my ribs," he said.

"Let me help. It's probably hard to do it yourself."

"Yes, but I don't need . . . " She was already in front of him taking the tape out of his hand. "Here, you hold the shirt in the right spot and I'll tape. Jeremy found some work gloves you can put on. They don't look very warm but they'll be better than nothing." She examined his side. "Wow, you have a terrible-looking bruise already. It's all black with some reddish purple bits. Hmmm . . . it sort of looks like a giant smashed beetle, like those pictures psychiatrists show you of blobs that you're supposed to identify. The blobs always look like bugs to me."

"Just tape, please." The bug talk confused him, and he didn't have the energy to ask her to explain. It was easier just to suffer in silent embarrassment by looking at a spot over the top of her head. She wound the tape around him once, pulling it so hard it felt like it was cutting into the skin of his back. "Ow! Does it have to be that tight?"

"I don't know," she said. "I've never had a role where I had to pretend to do first aid, but in the movies I've seen like this, the wounded one is supposed to suffer in silence. Then the camera moves in for a close-up of how stoic you are." She wrapped another section around him and tightened that, too. "There, that should hold," she said, ripping off the end of the tape.

"Ow! Very funny! I'm not feeling stoic, and those actors aren't really hurt, so it's not much of an effort to bite your lip and grimace."

"Like this?" Raine did a perfect imitation of an actor in pain, but in the process of striking a pose, she bumped into the wall of the trailer and a shower of snow fell on her.

"That wasn't bad," he said, reaching out to brush the snow off her face. Her cheek was so warm, he didn't want to take his hand away.

Jeremy stumbled in, tripping over a toolbox. "Stefan! Raine! Cecil's really sick!"

Chapter 16

SHELTER

Stefan grabbed the shirt and the tunic and pulled them on as he followed Raine and Jeremy. He realized the tape was working because he felt much better. "What's wrong with Cecil?"

"He's sweating and he's talking about stuff that doesn't make sense, like he's reciting lines from another movie. Hurry!"

They slogged back through the snow toward the fire and Cecil. Even from several feet away, Stefan could see the sheen of sweat on the old man's face. He sat staring at a bottle of pink-colored juice in his shaking hand like he was fascinated with the sloshing movement inside it. His other arm was around Kep, who was crouched in his lap.

"Cecil, are you okay?" Raine asked.

At the sound of her voice, he raised his head, his eyebrows furrowed as if he was surprised she had spoken. "'Feather of lead, bright smoke, cold fire, sick health! Still-waking sleep, that is not what it is!'" he mumbled. He turned to Stefan and said, "'Dost thou not laugh?'"

"Um, I don't know, Cecil." Stefan fell back a step, the alarm bells going off in his head.

Raine knelt down so her face was level with Cecil's and pointed at the bottle of juice. "Can you take a drink? It might make you feel better."

"Is he trying to tell us something?" Jeremy asked.

"I don't think so," Raine said. "He's quoting Shakespeare. It's some of Romeo's lines about love."

Cecil shifted the bottle into his other hand but didn't drink. "'Now is the winter of our discontent.'" He cackled a crazy laugh, then held up his arm like he was giving a toast.

"Okay, I don't like this," Stefan said. Cecil's confusion was making him seriously nervous.

"What's wrong with him?" Jeremy took hold of Stefan's sleeve. "Why isn't anyone here to help us? Aren't they worried we aren't answering our

183

phones?" His voice was pleading, like he expected Stefan to have answers.

Stefan didn't want to tell him what he thought. If the storm had disrupted cell phone service in the area by damaging a tower, no one would realize they weren't answering theirs because of the avalanche. They might be on their own for hours, maybe even overnight. The thought of facing cold and darkness was awful, especially with Cecil acting so strange.

"I don't know what's wrong with him, but it's too cold even by the fire," Stefan said, taking a stick and poking at it. "If you get too close, it's too hot, but then if you move away, not enough of you stays warm. If we had some shelter for Cecil, he'd feel better." The fire only flared briefly, then died back down. Stefan felt a moment of uneasiness. The bonfire had already consumed most of the wood that was easy to retrieve. If they ran out of wood, they were in big trouble, unless they managed to dig more out.

Raine adjusted the costume skins around Cecil. "We could try to help him climb down into the camera trailer. I don't know if he could get back out though, without a lot of help. I had to pull myself up by my arms and balance on one of the tipped over cameras."

Stefan didn't like the thought of getting Cecil down into a dark trailer partway buried in the snow. He didn't like the thought of going in it himself. The snow had picked up again and the trailer was probably already filling with snow anyway, because they hadn't done anything to cover the opening. The prop trailer wasn't really a choice either, unless they figured out some way to make the opening big enough for Cecil. They couldn't light a fire inside it either. He remembered the chemical odor he had smelled earlier. Whatever that had been, it was probably flammable.

"I'd rather try something else first," Stefan said.

"Maybe we can make a tent out of something," Jeremy said, "or a blanket fort out of the costume skins."

"There are tarps on the skimmers," Stefan said. "We could use those. Or he could just sit in one of the skimmers. It would at least get him under cover." He looked down at Cecil, who had lowered the bottle and was absently petting Kep's head.

"Then he wouldn't be close to a fire," Raine said. "Even if we built a new fire down by them, it wouldn't do him any good once he's inside one."

"Maybe we can use the tarps and the skins to

cover the open part of the equipment trailer." Even as Stefan said it, he knew it wasn't the best solution. The trailer was big, and it would take a lot of effort both to clear it out and then enclose it.

"We could build an igloo." Jeremy scooped up a handful of snow and tried to pack it together. "People stay warm in those."

Raine poked at the fire. "That's not very practical," she said. "Do you know how to build an igloo? I don't think we can just whip one up in a few minutes."

"Jeremy has the right idea." Stefan walked down the slope a few yards, trying to identify the various pieces of debris, trying to remember what exactly had been on the set. "I wish we still had the command outpost prop. That was like a small building." He didn't see anything at the spot where it had originally stood, but farther down there was a snow-covered mound of something lumpy enough to be man-made. "I think I see it."

"*I* still think we should get Cecil in the camera trailer," Raine said.

"Let's try this first. If it's really the command outpost, I'll need some help uncovering it." He glanced back at Cecil, hoping it was okay to leave him. The man was just staring off into space, but at least it was better than seeing him all agitated.

When they reached the mound, Stefan knelt down and brushed a small area clear, uncovering a section of black metal. From the etched design and the shimmering color, he knew it was part of the command building.

"Would you help me lift this up?" he asked Raine. Pulling one section free from the snow, they balanced it between them. With the snow off, he could see how they had been put together in the original building. Each piece was a curved pie-shaped wedge, taller than him, with hinges on both sides to fasten it to the next section.

"We can't put it all back together," Jeremy said, shifting another one. "Some of the hinges are broken."

"It doesn't have to be the full size. We can move some of these around so that we can make them into a little round shelter, like your igloo idea. Let's go through them to find the ones that still have hinges. If we don't find enough, we'll just tape them."

Some of the pieces were cracked and missing chunks, but the rest of them were mostly whole. "I think we should drag them back so we're close to the fire," Stefan said. They weren't heavy, and it didn't take long to fasten what they had together. The sections didn't fit snugly next to each other where they curved to form the ceiling. When Raine pointed that out, Stefan said, "We'll throw a tarp over the top, but we can leave a small opening for smoke, and then we'll build a fire inside."

When they were finished, they had a shelter about the size of a large camping tent. Stefan couldn't find the door piece to the outpost, so he used one of the costume skins as a flap over the opening, taping it along the top and securing the creature head above the door so it would be out of the way. It gave a weird-looking tribal feel to the structure, like the creature was a hunting trophy, or a warning sign not to enter. Inside, there wasn't much room to move around, but Stefan figured they didn't need any. Besides, the closer they were together, he reasoned, the warmer they would be. It was very dark inside, like being deep underground.

"This is terrific!" Raine said. "I can't believe we made something so great."

Stefan observed their work, trying to figure out what else they needed to do. "Jeremy, would you go get one of those stunt mattresses you found?

Did you see an air pump to blow them up?"

"I don't know what an air pump looks like."

"They hook them up to special fans to inflate the air bags," Raine said. "But we don't have any way to plug in the fans."

"So much for the pump. Just get the mattress. At least it will be a barrier between Cecil and the wet snow."

"I'll get some more wood for a fire," Raine said.

"Why don't you help me with Cecil first?" He hoped the man wouldn't start quoting lines again. Seeing someone that confused was almost worse than seeing them physically ill.

Cecil and Kep were both dozing. Phoebe sat next to them, trying to lick the wound on her neck.

"Should we wake him up?" Raine whispered. "I wish we knew what was wrong with him."

"Whatever it is, he'll be better off out of the snow." Stefan gently shook Cecil's arm. "Wake up, Cecil." The man opened his eyes but didn't speak. "When you warm up, you'll feel better," Stefan said, more to convince himself than Cecil.

Raine picked up Kep and then put him on the ground. The little dog whined and acted as if he was going to try to jump back into Cecil's lap.

"Just wait a minute," Raine said. "Once we get

Cecil inside, you can have your spot again." Stefan was glad to see the pug had stopped shivering.

"I'll help Cecil if you bring the chair," Stefan said. He took the costume skins off Cecil and then urged the old man out of the chair. Taking Cecil's arm and putting it over his shoulder, Stefan supported him as they shuffled down the hill. Phoebe and Kep came with them, but Boris and Natasha ignored them, still circling around the set and sniffing the ground.

Raine darted ahead with the chair and disappeared inside. As soon as she was out of sight, Kep barked and ran after her. Phoebe followed right behind him. Stefan didn't understand why the wolf had gotten so attached to the little dog, but he supposed that would be something for a wolf expert, not him, to figure out.

Before Cecil and Stefan were even halfway to the shelter, Raine was back outside. "I'd like to go put on one of the costumes. I'm really cold in these clothes. I'll bring a tunic for Cecil, if there's one that looks like it will fit him. Are you okay, or do you need some help?"

Stefan had been so occupied with Cecil, he hadn't noticed Raine was still wearing the same snow-caked clothes she'd had on since the avalanche. "We're okay," he said, even though his side hurt more with Cecil's extra weight dragging on him.

By the time he finally got Cecil inside, Jeremy had already laid out two air mattresses. Phoebe and Kep were curled up on one. "They're really big," the boy said, "so I didn't need to unfold them all the way. It's better that way, because the folded layers make them more comfortable, like they are real mattresses."

Stefan didn't think they looked comfortable at all, but they couldn't be choosy.

"What should I do now?" Jeremy asked cheerfully.

"Why don't you go get the costume skins? I left them by the fire. Cecil, would you rather lie down or sit in the chair?" Stefan asked. Cecil nodded at the chair, so Stefan helped him over to it.

Raine, in a dry costume now, pushed through the flap carrying a crumpled piece of metal. "I had a great idea! I don't know what this was, but I found this in the kitchen area. We can make a fire in it like it's a mini patio fire bowl so it won't go out from the snow melting. The bonfire is already dying down from the snow melting underneath it." She grinned, clearly very pleased with her plan.

"Good idea," Stefan said. "I'll help you find some wood."

They gathered up what small pieces they could find. Without an ax it would be hard to break up the larger pieces into something they could use inside the shelter. There were plenty of broken trees around, but Stefan knew green wood from fresh trees wouldn't burn well.

Jeremy joined them. "I ran and got a tunic for Cecil and then I helped him wrap up in the costume skins. He's getting warm, so I came to help you."

"Good, we can use the help," Stefan said. "Pick up anything small enough to fit in the fire in the shelter."

Boris and Natasha were nosing around in the debris by the kitchen. Natasha had dug up a piece of meat, something that from a distance looked like a steak. She crouched down to gnaw on it, growling when Boris came over to investigate. Seeing Stefan watching her, she got up and loped off into the trees, still carrying the meat. Boris started to dig at the spot Natasha had abandoned.

"What do you think he's digging up?" Raine asked.

"Meat," Stefan said. "Wolves don't eat anything else. He's not going to hunt for lentil soup."

"Very funny," Raine said. "That might deserve a snowball." She focused back on Boris instead. "You don't think . . . it couldn't be . . . the cook?"

"NO!" Stefan said, irritated she had brought up the cook in front of Jeremy.

"The cook?" Jeremy looked stricken. "I forgot about her. Where is she?"

"I think the cook must have gone home last night," Stefan said. "We looked for her this morning and didn't find her. I'm sure Boris just smells more steaks or whatever they had in the refrigerator."

"Are you sure?" Jeremy asked.

Stefan noticed Jeremy's breaths were getting a little squeaky. "I'm sure. You have your inhaler, right?" he asked.

"No, it was inside the lodge." The boy took a few deep breaths like he was experimenting with breathing. They could all hear the wheezing. "I'm okay, except I forgot to take the medicine I was supposed to take last night. My dad is the one who always reminds me. But if someone gets here soon, I'll be fine." He coughed and the wheezing sounded louder.

Stefan tried to stay calm, but he didn't know if he could deal with both Cecil and Jeremy getting sick. Neither Raine nor Jeremy seemed to realize just how bad things were. It was like they thought they were actually just acting in a movie, pretending they were in danger, but telling themselves they really weren't. He knew, even if they didn't, they were all in serious trouble, and things were likely to get worse. He didn't think they should count on people making a quick rescue attempt.

He made a decision. "We need to go for help," he said. Saying it made him feel better. He had to do something. "If I can get down the cliff using the cables, I could walk down the lower part of the mountain to the village." He tried to figure out how many hours it would take. Was there enough time before dark? His ribs ached at the thought of the climb and the walk, but it didn't seem like there was much choice.

"No, it's too far in the snow for either one of us. If we had some skis or snowboards, it wouldn't be so hard, but we'd never be able to walk all that way. I have a better idea." Raine pulled the crumpled map from her pocket and smoothed it out. "I was looking at this while I was waiting for Jeremy. We're here," she said, pointing, "and the closest labeled place is this Castle Ruil. It doesn't look very far. See? Maybe it's just right over there." She pointed off beyond the lodge to the west, where a forest of spruce trees covered a relatively flat area that rose in the distance to another mountain. "Our mountain makes up one side of a bowl, just like a lot of the really good ski resorts at home, and this castle looks like it has to be on the other side of the bowl before the elevation starts to rise again."

Stefan tried to remember what the area had looked like before the snow started. He knew he hadn't seen any castle, but maybe the trees were just obscuring it.

"If it's on the map, that means there are people there, right?" Raine said.

Taking the map from her, he found the spot. "I don't know. I didn't even know there were castles in Slovakia."

"There are lots of them, but they're small, more like stone manor houses. I read about it in a guide book. I guess people liked to call them castles."

"How far away is it?" The snowflakes were already blotching up the map with wet marks, making it tough to see specific features or the key.

Raine used her fingers to measure. "Only a half mile or so."

"I thought you said there weren't any roads

close to us. If it's only a half mile, that could be good. We can handle that." He studied the map more carefully. "But I don't see a road going to it. If someone lived there, it would have a road."

"Maybe the road isn't big enough to be on the map. Like it's a private road just to the castle."

Stefan didn't know what to do. He didn't want to be the one to make the decision. But if they didn't do anything, and Cecil got worse, then it might be too late to do anything. "Okay, I'll go," he said. "You stay here and watch out for them."

She grabbed the map back from him. "Don't treat me like a girl. I'll go. You're the one who's hurt, and it was my idea anyway."

"You should both go, so you can help each other. What if you were by yourself and you got lost? I can watch out for Cecil," Jeremy said.

Stefan was surprised Jeremy didn't seem scared at the idea of staying without them.

The kid didn't seem to understand he wouldn't be able to do anything if Cecil got worse, even though when Stefan thought about it, it wasn't like he or Raine knew what to do either.

"We might both get lost," Stefan argued.

"Jeremy's right," Raine said. "In all the movies I've ever seen, the one who goes off by himself never comes back. Terrible things happen to them. That's when the crazy people or the monsters get them."

Stefan didn't like where this discussion was going. "Fine, but I'm not exactly worried about an abominable snowman jumping out at us. We need to get moving if we're going to do this. It will be slow walking through all that snow."

"What about our wolves?" Jeremy said. "They're staying here, right?"

"Right," Stefan said. "If we show up at someone's house with a pack of wolves, they won't be happy to see us."

"I wasn't thinking about that," Jeremy said. "If that wolf you saw yesterday comes back, I want Boris here. He looks tough and he could chase it off."

"We shouldn't chance it. Maybe you shouldn't let either of the wolves run free. Our guys might get hurt in a fight with an untamed wolf," Raine said. "These wolves don't even know how to live in the wild. It's our fault they can't take care of themselves, I mean, not us, right here, right now, but it's someone's fault they're more like dogs than wolves."

"I didn't think about them getting hurt. I'll tie

them up and keep them close to me," Jeremy said.

"Just make sure Kep doesn't get too cold either," Raine said. "He doesn't realize he doesn't have as much fur as a wolf."

"I'll take care of everyone," Jeremy said. "We'll be fine."

Stefan hoped so. Even though Jeremy acted a little young for his age, the kid didn't seem the kind to do anything too stupid.

"Okay," Stefan said. "Let's go then."

"No, wait, we need some supplies." Raine ran past the rapidly shrinking fire to a cooler and opened the lid. "Do you want something to drink?" she asked, pulling out a bottle of juice the same peach color of Cecil's. "It's carrot papaya nectar; that's the only kind in the cooler."

"No food?" He'd give anything for one of those plum dumplings.

She shook her head. "Just juice. I thought I had found another cooler, but it was only a lid."

Stefan sighed. "Okay, it's better than nothing." Taking the bottle, he drank it all, unable to stop himself. Even though he was still only slightly warmer than frozen, his mouth was parched, and the sweetness of the juice immediately made him feel better.

"We can probably survive on this for days if we have to," Raine said. "People in the wilderness live on bugs and atrocious stuff like that. At least we have something with vitamins in it."

"There's no way I'm sitting around for days in the cold with only carrot papaya juice as nourishment, no matter how many vitamins it has." The thought of a juice diet was enough incentive to get him moving. "Jeremy, you should go inside," he said, still not sure about leaving the kid behind. He'd feel better knowing Jeremy and Cecil were under cover, out of the snow. He felt more flakes on his face and brushed at them. When they were busy doing things, he could almost forget about the snow, but every time he stopped to think, there was no way to ignore it.

"Go on!" Jeremy waved at them. "We'll be fine."

"Come on, Stefan," Raine said.

As soon as they got beyond the set area into undisturbed snow, they immediately sank way down into the powder with each step. The novelty of making tracks through unbroken snow wore off before they even reached the trees. Stefan hoped the castle was only a half mile away. He tried to remember how many feet were in a mile, and then started to count his steps as a way to keep moving. Every ten steps was an accomplishment, and a hundred an even greater one.

"I just realized the people at the castle probably won't speak English," Raine said. "How are we going to explain what we need?"

"I don't know. Can you draw? Maybe we can draw an old man lying down, or something. We can do a lot of pointing or miming. Or you can do the miming, you're the actor. Act out Cecil getting sick."

"I can do that," Raine said. "That was scary when he was babbling those lines."

Stefan didn't answer. He had lost count of his footsteps and was getting too winded to talk. They trudged on until they were surrounded by trees. The narrow spruces were so covered with snow, they looked like weird sculptures. It was totally silent, probably because any birds or animals were smart enough to be curled up somewhere warm, unlike dumb humans. Maybe they should have stayed at the shelter.

The forest ended abruptly at a small cliff face of jumbled boulders. From where they stood, it appeared that the ground leveled off on top before it started to rise again. Stefan didn't see any castle, but it was possible there was something up above on the level part. The cliff wasn't nearly as tall or as steep as the one by the lodge, and in normal circumstances, in good weather, it would have been easy to climb.

"Before we do this, are you sure we're going in the right direction?" Stefan asked.

"I'm sure," Raine said. "I'm very good at reading maps."

Stefan lifted his arm up, trying to find a handhold, but a sharp jolt of pain went through him. He tried to use his other arm on his good side, and it didn't hurt as much, but after a few feet he had to stop. Whatever he had done to his ribs, climbing wasn't good for them. Raine was already picking her way up a few feet beyond him. She didn't seem like she was having any trouble.

"Raine, my side is really hurting. When you get to the top, tell me if you can see the castle and then I'll try to come up." As Raine scrambled up the cliff, snow cascaded down each time she moved, like mini avalanches. Stefan moved back to avoid getting plastered with more snow. When he looked up again, Raine had disappeared over the top.

"Do you see it?" Stefan called.

When she didn't answer, he called again. It

would be just their luck if the place was empty, or closed up for the winter. Maybe it would be okay to break in and get some supplies. They could leave a note and offer to pay.

Her face appeared over the top. He could tell from her grim expression something was wrong.

"It's just the ruins of a castle," she said. "Don't bother coming up. There are some broken-down walls, nothing else." More snow fell in front of her as she started down. "Sorry. I guess it was a bad idea to walk all the way here."

Stefan was about to answer when he was distracted by a flash of movement behind a boulder to Raine's right. A wolf, the bloody leg of a rabbit in its mouth, stood watching her.

Chapter 17

WATCHERS

The wolf's fur was gray and matted; the creature so thin, every rib showed. It stared at Raine with an unwavering gaze, blood dripping from the thing in its mouth onto the snow. Stefan knew Raine didn't see it.

"Now you are supposed to say something like 'It's okay,' instead of standing there like a statue," she said.

"Raine." The word came out as a whisper, so Stefan tried again. "Raine, get down here as fast as you can. There's a wolf up there and it's watching you."

She started and twisted around. "Where?"

"To your right. Don't waste time looking for it,

just come on down." He looked around, trying to find a loose rock to throw if it came any closer. There were lots of boulders, but the ground around him was so covered with snow, he didn't see any rocks. The way his ribs ached, he didn't know how far he'd be able to throw a stone any-way. The wolf still hadn't moved. It was almost as if it didn't want Raine to notice it. He hoped the animal was afraid of her.

Raine took a few steps forward and the wolf just watched.

"Keep moving," Stefan said. "The wolf isn't doing anything."

She was about three feet down when another wolf loomed behind her, as silent as the first. Stefan somehow knew it was the same one that had been on the set. It was bigger than the other and so thin, it was like looking at a skeleton cov-ered with fur. When it turned toward him, Stefan gasped at the sight of the wolf's head. Part of the skin on the right side of its muzzle was missing, like it had been ripped off. The fangs, stained with dried blood, were exposed as if the wolf had a permanent sneer on its face. And there was something wrong with its right eye. It wasn't the glowing yellow of the other; it had a white cast to it, like it was covered in film.

"Move a little faster, Raine," Stefan said. He didn't want to tell her about the other wolf, in case the sight of it startled her so much she fell.

The urgency in his words sent her sliding down the hill. Stefan reached out an arm to catch her. The white-eyed wolf moved silently to the spot where Raine had been standing, sniffing the ground while he watched them. The other wolf had disappeared.

Raine looked back up at the cliff and gave a muffled shriek.

"Let's go," Stefan said, trying to drag her away by her coat sleeve. "I don't think they're going to come straight down the cliff like you did."

"What's wrong with that wolf?" She shuddered. "Its eye and its mouth were terrible."

"I don't know about the eye, but it looks like it was injured in a fight. I'm amazed it's alive with its mouth like that."

"Do you think they are going to come after us?"

Stefan looked back. The wolf still stood at the top of the cliff, just watching.

"No, Hans said they avoid people. I think we just stumbled on where they live. They were really skinny too. I don't know if they'd have the energy to chase us."

"I feel kind of bad for them even if they are horrible looking. How can they be so thin and still be alive?"

"Maybe it's been a hard winter." The thought flashed through his mind, but he didn't speak it: *If they are really skinny, then they are really hungry.* "Let's just keep walking." He looked back again. The wolf was gone. Just emptiness remained where it had been standing, emptiness and snow. That should have made him feel better, but instead he felt a sudden burst of fear. An unseen wolf could be anywhere, tracking them, watching them. Between the trees and the snowfall and the silent way the creatures moved, Stefan knew he wouldn't be able to tell if a wolf was after them until it had already ambushed them. His heart racing, he moved his head from side to side, trying to spot any movement in the trees. Nothing.

He couldn't see the set either, and tried to tell himself they weren't close enough yet. It wouldn't be visible until they moved beyond the trees. He wished now he had kept count of his steps so he'd know how much farther they had to go.

Raine was moving faster than he was and she stopped, waiting for him to catch up. "You know,

I read this book last year," she said, "and there was a story in it about hungry wolves chasing a line of sleds. The people in the front sleds could hear the other ones being overtaken by wolves and they just kept going. They were glad the ones in the back were sacrificed."

"Okay, not a good topic of conversation." Stefan looked back over his shoulder and then wished he hadn't. The wolf was trailing behind them. It wasn't moving as if it were trying to catch up, but it was definitely tracking them, keeping a fixed distance between them. Grabbing Raine's arm, he said, "Let's walk a little faster. There's a wolf behind us." So much for Hans's assurances. This wolf wasn't scared of them.

"Is it the one with the eye?" She twisting around and he lost his grip on her.

"I think so," he said. He couldn't see well through the snow, but he just knew it was the white-eyed wolf.

"We should run," Raine said.

"No, remember they are afraid of people. If we run, they'll think we are prey. Just keep walking."

"How do you know that?"

"I don't, but it just makes sense." He was more concerned with sighting only one wolf. If there was the one he could see, where was the other?

The wolf was still there, not hurrying, keeping an even distance from them, his eyes fixed on them. "We'll walk side by side so no one will be the sacrificial wolf chow," Stefan said. "Don't tell that story to Jeremy, okay? You don't believe everything you read, do you? It was just a story."

"Even if it was just a story, a lot of stories are based on real things. Something like that could have happened," she insisted.

"Don't you read any books that aren't so dramatic . . . like . . . I don't know . . . clumsy girl makes the basketball team, or something like that?"

"No. Are there books like that?"

"I don't know. Probably." He tried to think of another subject, anything to keep their minds off the wolves, but the image of the white-eyed one wouldn't stay out of his head.

"You know, this isn't so much fun anymore," Raine said.

Stefan had to laugh. "You call surviving an avalanche fun? I haven't been having fun for quite a while now."

"No, I mean the power going out, and us being in the lodge by ourselves, well, almost by ourselves, and then actually surviving the avalanche and rescuing Jeremy and Cecil. It all felt great, in a weird way, like we were really doing something, instead of always just pretending to do something. In acting, it's all so fake. People who have seen my movies think I know how to skydive and walk on tightropes and skate like an Olympian. I can't do any of that. It's all stunt people. I just pretend I'm getting ready to do those things, and then when the stunt people are done, I act like it was me all along. For once we were doing real things, but now it's getting a little scary. No stunt double is here to face off with a wolf."

"We're not going to have to do that." He said it to reassure both of them, but he wasn't sure he believed it. Why was the wolf in plain sight as if it didn't care that they saw him? Stefan had a bad feeling about the one with the white eye. His grandfather had taught him to always beware of a wild animal that didn't act wild. He could almost hear his grandfather's voice: *If you see a wild creature who isn't scared of you, be scared of it. An animal like that is sure to be sick, maybe even with rabies, and a sick creature is an irrational one. Get away as fast as you can.*

He wished they could move faster, but the

snow was so deep, his leg muscles were burning with the effort to raise and lower them enough to move forward. They came out of the trees and Stefan could see some faint shapes of the set in the distance, like a mirage wavering in the blowing snow.

"It's gone!" Raine pointed behind them, and all Stefan could see were the trees and their own rapidly disappearing footprints.

"I hope it stays gone," Stefan said, wondering why it had been following them in the first place.

From a distance, the set looked desolate. The bonfire was mostly out. Gray smoke rose in wisps above the blackened boards. He tried to slow down his breathing enough to stop the sharp pain that came every time he took a deep breath. "Go ahead. I'll be there in a minute."

As soon as they were on firmer snow, Raine ran ahead into the shelter. She came right back out. "Jeremy!" she yelled. "Do you see him?" she said as she came back toward Stefan. "Cecil sounds better, but he said he was dozing when Jeremy went out. He doesn't remember when."

Stefan scanned the area. "He's wearing the costume tunic, right? The black should stand out against all this white." He didn't see any black blotch. Where could the kid go? "Let's look by the lodge."

He almost missed him. Jeremy sat on top of a pile of stones next to the top of a broken tree, his head bowed. The kid looked so tiny and alone out in the middle of nowhere, like he had been left in an abandoned battlefield.

"Jeremy!" Stefan called. The boy didn't look up; he just rocked back and forth, clutching something in his hand. "Raine, he's up here."

As they drew close to him, Raine yanked Stefan back, pointing right beyond Jeremy. The white-eyed wolf stood about ten feet beyond the boy, perfectly still, staring at Jeremy. It turned its head to them, the yellow eye fixed as if it was challenging them to make a move. It kept shaking its head in a strange way, like it was trying to get something off itself. Every few seconds it would snap at the air and growl. Stefan could tell the wolf had no fear of them. He backed up slowly, pulling Raine with him. How had it gotten in front of them? How could it move so silently?

"Jeremy!" Raine yelled. The boy still didn't look up.

"I think his foot is stuck," Stefan said. He could see one of Jeremy's boots, but the other was partly covered by some of the rubble.

"Jeremy!" Raine yelled again.

Stefan felt sick watching the wolf. Now that he was closer, he could see how the white eye more clearly. The pupil behind the film didn't track with the other eye; it was like it was locked into place, dead and unseeing. "There's something really wrong with that wolf," Stefan said.

"We have to chase it away," Raine whispered.

"Fire," Stefan said. "We'll use fire." He started edging back to the smoking fire, walking backward so he could keep the wolf in sight. A chorus of howls came from behind him and he was so surprised he stumbled. "Are our wolves inside the igloo?"

"It looks like Jeremy tied Boris and Phoebe up. Natasha's not there. I was going to untie them once we found him. Should we get them? Maybe they can scare off the wolf."

Stefan wasn't sure the white-eyed wolf was scared of anything. "We can try. I guess it's two against one. Hurry! I'll get some burning wood."

The fire was down to almost nothing, and Stefan kicked the charred pieces that remained, trying to find something he could pick up. Everything was either crumbled into charcoal or too hot to touch. He'd have to find some new wood to light. He heard a strangled sound from Raine. When he turned to look at her she was trying to speak, but he couldn't make out her words.

He took her by the shoulders, dreading to hear what she was trying to say. "Take a breath so you can talk. What's wrong? Is it Cecil?"

"No . . . There are two more wolves, wild wolves, right outside the shelter." She took a few more deep breaths of air. "I can't get inside and when I yelled to Cecil, he didn't answer, or if he did, I couldn't hear him. Our wolves are going crazy in there growling and barking. I think they're trying to get out."

"We have to help Jeremy first. Try to find another piece of wood and light it. I'm going to see if there's something in the prop trailer to help us." He raced back to the trailer, running through possibilities in his mind. Once inside he shoved things out of the way until he spotted the case with the tanto weapons. He buckled one of them on his arm and extended it, tucking the other in his pocket. He found the pile of ice spiders and picked some up, clamped them along the tanto blade, then gathered as many more as he could carry. He hoped they all still worked.

Back outside Raine was pushing a board into the fire. "I can't get the wood to light!" she yelled.

"I've got something else. Hurry! We need to get back to Jeremy."

He explained as they went, his words coming in jagged bursts of sound.

The wolf had moved a few feet closer to Jeremy, his eyes intent on the boy, but Jeremy seemed oblivious to the danger. Stefan feared the wolf was trying work up its nerve to leap at him.

"When I count to three, switch on your costume so it glows," Stefan said. "Then start hitting the buttons on the ice spiders. Be ready because they're going to make a terrible noise." He took as deep a breath as he could manage. "One, two, three. Now!"

They charged the wolf, pushing the buttons on the ice spiders as they ran. The shrieking mechanical creatures were so loud Stefan knew he was yelling but couldn't hear himself. When they were close enough, Stefan launched one of them at the wolf and then the other. Raine added hers to the fray, putting a twist on her throws so that the spiders tumbled over and over in the air.

The wolf turned on them and snarled, baring its teeth. It crouched down and Stefan was afraid it was going to attack, but then its nerve broke, and it fell back, crouching low to the ground, snapping at the air. Finally it gave one last snarl and sprinted off into the trees.

Stefan was about to sink to the ground when a loud growl erupted behind them. He turned to see Phoebe rolling around on the ground with the two wild wolves, snapping and snarling. One wolf bit down on her and she gave a yelp of pain. Stefan could hear Boris inside barking frantically.

Pulling a spider off the blade, he threw it at the wolves, but they were so engaged in the battle, none of them noticed. Phoebe was bleeding heavily. She went down and the other two wolves were on her. A deep cry came from the shelter as Cecil burst out, carrying a torch, the costume skin wrapped around him so that the monster head loomed about his own. The man let out a deep-voiced roar, waving the torch, like an ancient shaman chasing away demons. The remaining two wolves didn't even attempt to take a stand. They dashed after the white-eyed wolf, and Cecil collapsed onto the ground.

Chapter 18

DARKNESS

Stefan ran to him. Cecil was breathing heavily, but he smiled as he looked up. "I can still do an action scene when called for," he gasped. "Is Phoebe alive?"

When Stefan checked on her, he could see the wolf was breathing. The cut on her neck had reopened and she had a new gash on her back. She whined and then got to her feet, her eyes darting back and forth like she was afraid she would be attacked again.

"Stefan, help me!" Raine yelled.

Stefan realized he had forgotten about Jeremy for a minute. "Are you okay?" he asked Cecil.

The old man waved a hand. "Go, I'm just

getting my breath back."

Raine was on her knees shaking Jeremy. "Jeremy, wake up!"

The boy's lips were blue and he was shivering so hard it looked like his body was moving in ripples. He opened his eyes, but Stefan could tell he wasn't really seeing them.

"Let me go to sleep," he said. "I'll be warmer if I go sleep."

"No! Jeremy, you have to get up!" Stefan reached down to try to pull him to his feet. Raine had already freed Jeremy's foot.

"What's wrong with him?" Raine asked. "Is it something to do with the asthma?"

"No, it's a sign of hypothermia. I've heard my mother talk about seeing cases at the hospital. We have to get him warm."

"What was he doing out here? We shouldn't have left him alone!"

"Let's get him inside."

They took the boy between them and helped him back to the shelter, passing Phoebe, who was licking her wounds.

"She looks bad," Raine said.

"We'll come help her once we get Jeremy inside." Jeremy was walking without a problem, but he didn't speak; he just let out an occasional sniffle.

Cecil was already back huddled under the costume skins, and even though he was breathing strangely, Stefan was happy to see he looked almost normal. Boris was gnawing at the cord that was fastened to his collar. Someone, Cecil or Jeremy, had pounded a pole into the ground and tied the wolf and Kep to it, using some shorter extension cords as makeshift leashes.

"What's wrong with the boy?" Cecil asked.

"His foot got trapped and he got too cold." Stefan tried to remember his mother's stories about how they treated kids who fell through ice or got lost in the woods in the winter, but he couldn't think of any details besides getting them warm. "Here, Raine, can you sit with him and wrap your arms around him? I'll cover you both up and then build up the fire."

"Put something on his head," Cecil said. "He's losing too much heat that way."

Stefan saw that the stunt mattresses had been partly inflated. He didn't know how they had managed, but this wasn't the right time to figure it out. The mattresses made the shelter look a little more comfortable, and he knew Jeremy would get warmer more quickly if he was off the cold ground. While they were getting the boy all bundled up, Phoebe hobbled in and lay down next to Boris. When Kep saw her he began yelping and straining at the cord that held him until Stefan untied him. The little dog immediately ran to Phoebe and pushed himself under her chin.

"How bad is she?" Raine asked.

Stefan moved a little closer to the wolf, but he didn't want to crowd her. If she was hurt, she might overreact. "I don't know. She's not bleeding too much."

"At least she's safe now. Those wolves will be too scared to come back," Raine said.

Stefan wasn't so sure. He feared the white-eyed wolf would be back.

It took some time, but finally Jeremy grew more alert. The rest of them sat quietly watching him until his sniffles turned into big gasping sobs. "That wolf was going to get me!"

"I don't think so, Jeremy. It was just watching you," Raine said reassuringly.

"Where's Natasha?" Jeremy said, trying to stand up. "Has she come back? I tied up the other wolves because I didn't want them running away like her."

"Jeremy, stay covered up!" Stefan ordered.

"You have to get warm. We haven't seen Natasha. I think she likes being free."

"But how can she leave Boris and Phoebe? They're part of her pack."

"I don't know. Maybe the idea of freedom was stronger."

They were all silent. The wind blowing through the cracks in the shelter panels sounded like alien music, weird and lonely.

"Did you find help?" Jeremy asked. "Is someone coming to get us?"

"No, it was just the ruins of a castle," Stefan said. That already seemed so long ago. "There wasn't anybody there." He felt really worn out now, thinking of all they had been through that day. The knowledge they'd still be there when night fell didn't make him happy.

"I'm hungry," Raine said.

"Did you get the sausages?" Jeremy asked. "I found some up the hill. Well, Boris found some, a lot, and I took the ones he didn't eat. Where'd they go?"

"Sausages?" Stefan said.

"I had them in my hand when I slipped and my foot got stuck," Jeremy said.

Stefan remembered Jeremy had been clutching

something in his hand, but he didn't remember seeing anything after the wolves had been chased off. He went back outside and it only took a minute to find the package, six sausages wrapped in white paper. No wonder the wolf had been so close to Jeremy. It wasn't interested in him, it smelled the sausages. If Jeremy had just thrown them to the wolf, the creature might have gone away happy. Now that they had them though, there was no reason not to eat them. Stefan broke off some smaller branches from one of the downed trees to use as skewers for the meat and then took everything inside.

Once the sausages were cooking over the fire, Stefan didn't think anything had ever smelled as tantalizing. He could hardly restrain his impatience but he waited until the fire had crisped the skin of his, turning it to a golden brown. When he bit into it, it burned his mouth. He didn't care. It was delicious. One of the wolves whined and he looked up to find them and Kep staring intently at the sausage.

He felt a twinge of guilt as he took another bite. "Didn't you guys already scarf up all the extra meat?" Stefan asked the animals. "How hungry can you be?"

"We have to give them some," Raine said, taking an extra sausage and breaking it into pieces. "They don't want just frozen raw meat. Gross." She fed a bit to each one.

"Now I know why wild wolves in stories are so awful," Jeremy said.

"Not all wolves in stories are bad. What about the wolves who took care of Mowgli in *The Jungle Book*? They were good wolves." Raine broke her stick into pieces and added it to the fire. It was too green to catch well.

"That's just one story."

"I know another. I'll tell it to you if you think about going to sleep. It's getting dark and I'm getting tired."

"What's it called?" Jeremy asked.

"It's the actual true story about Little Red Riding Hood. You know, even though wolves aren't naturally bad, some people are, and Little Red was one of those people, really bad."

Jeremy already looked like his attention was caught. He stopped sniffling.

Stefan went to the door. Between the fading daylight and the heavy snowfall he couldn't see far enough through the opening, but he knew the wolves were still out there. Boris came over and pushed in front of him, like he was nudging Stefan back into the shelter.

He heard Raine's voice switch to a singsong tone. "Once upon a time there was a small kingdom high in the mountains where everyone lived happily raising cows and making cheese, but next to this kingdom, there lived a bad outlaw who was planning to invade it. He wanted to take over the cheese production, and he recruited Little Red to help him."

"This sounds like a silly story," Jeremy said. "I'm too old for ones like that."

"Just wait. It gets more exciting. Little Red Riding Hood wasn't a little girl, she was a very short grown-up. She worked in the kitchen at the castle as a dishwasher, but she also worked for the outlaw. The grandmother lived in the kingdom and she was a real grandmother, just not Little Red's grandmother. She lived in a broken-down hut deep in the woods."

"Why was the hut broken?" Jeremy asked.

"I don't know. It doesn't matter."

"She could fix the hut," he insisted.

"She was old and her hands were all gnarled up with arthritis. She couldn't fix the hut. Anyway, the grandmother was a spy too. Little Red would visit her, pretending to bring baskets of food so she could pass information on about what was happening in the kingdom. The grandmother would pass on the information to the outlaw to help him plan his invasion."

Stefan tried to think of what they should do when daylight came. If the snow stopped by then and the cell phones still weren't working, surely someone would try to find a way across the river to come check on them. At least he hoped they would.

Raine's voice drew him back into her story. She did have a nice voice when she wanted to use it. "Now the queen of this kingdom didn't trust anyone. She'd grown up surrounded by people who just pretended to like her because she was the queen."

Jeremy interrupted again. "Where was the king?"

"There was no king. The queen was in charge. Do you want me to finish this story or not?" Jeremy nodded his head. "Good, no more questions then. She knew the outlaw wanted to take over her kingdom and she suspected someone in the castle was feeding him information. Her only chance was to hire a lone wolf who naturally wouldn't be working for anyone, because lone wolves just don't do that. She found a big gray wolf named Silvertip. He had gray fur that was almost white on the tips, so he looked like he had been dipped in silver.

"Once the queen had explained what she wanted, the wolf said, 'Why would I want to work with you? I'm a lone wolf and I'm not crazy about humans.'"

"Like Natasha," Jeremy said.

"Right, like Natasha, she's not much of a life-of-the-party wolf. Well, this wolf was like her.

"The queen said, 'If the outlaw takes over, he'll hunt you down and use your pelt for a rug.'" Jeremy gasped. "'You need to work for me to make sure that doesn't happen. Now somewhere in the woods is a spy, and I want you to find him or her and neutralize them.'

"The wolf decided he would do what she wanted, because he didn't want to become a rug. He cruised around the forest pretending to be an ordinary wolf so he could track down the spy. He grew suspicious of Little Red almost immediately because he noticed she only skipped when other people were watching. As soon as she was alone, she would stop and take a break to smoke a cigarette.

"The wolf discovered the grandmother, and the queen's soldiers came to get her. The wolf decided to disguise himself as the grandmother to capture Little Red. The spy came in with her basket of food and they went through the whole bit of 'what big eyes you have,' etc., etc. Then the wolf said, 'I've heard the invasion is tomorrow. Go back and get ready to open the gate when the invasion starts.'

"The wolf followed Little Red back to the castle and told the queen. Little Red was arrested and thrown in the dungeon with the grandmother. The kingdom was saved. The wolf thought about going back to being a lone wolf, but then he decided that was kind of a lonely life, so he became the queen's trusted advisor, and they all lived happily ever after. The end."

There was silence except for the crackling of the fire, and then Cecil said, "It worked. The boy's asleep." They listened to the sound of Jeremy's wheezy breathing. "Nicely done, Miss Randolph. You have a true actor's voice, mesmerizing when you engage your audience. I see a great future for you on the stage, if you so choose."

"Where did that story come from?" Stefan asked.

"I made it up." She shrugged. "That's not the real ending, though. I'd have the invasion happen anyway and then there would be a colossal battle and the queen would charge out on her horse and slay all her enemies. More exciting that way."

No one spoke for a few minutes. Stefan watched the flickering fire, thinking if he stared at it long enough, it might put him to sleep.

Raine picked up Kep. "Toto, we're not in Kansas anymore," she murmured.

"Do you like *The Wizard of Oz*?" Stefan asked. His brothers loved it when he did whole sections of the movie for them, saying the lines of all the characters.

"Like it? I'm crazy about it. That's when I decided I wanted to be an actress, the first time I saw it. I was only four though, and for a long time I was very scared of the part with the wicked witch and the flying monkeys."

"Oh, the witch role was a wonderful part." Cecil chuckled. "Margaret Hamilton played it perfectly, though I always felt sorry for her having to wear that dreadful green makeup."

"I do a good wicked witch imitation," Stefan said, but as soon as the words were out of his mouth, he couldn't believe he had told them. Only his family had seen that one.

"You're kidding!" Raine put Kep down. "I want to hear it!"

"It's actually not that good." Stefan wanted to kick himself. "In fact, it's pretty bad. Besides, it will wake up Jeremy."

"Now don't be shy, Stefan," Cecil said. "You can do it softly. I'd like to hear the imitation too."

They badgered him a little longer until Stefan finally gave in, just to make them stop.

"Okay, but I'm just going to do the bit where Dorothy throws water on the witch. Those are the best lines." He stood up and hunched over a little, then cleared his throat and concentrated on getting the voice right. Glaring at Raine like she was Dorothy he cackled, "'You cursed brat! Look what you've done! I'm melting! I'm melting! Oh, what a world! Who would have thought a good little girl like you could destroy my beautiful wickedness? Oooooh, look out! I'm going! Oooooh! Ooooooh!'" He sank to the ground like he had melted away.

"Bravo!" Cecil said, clapping quietly.

"That was good." Raine got up. "Can you do the Cowardly Lion? I can do the Scarecrow."

Just then Boris jumped up and very slowly

stalked to the door, growling softly. The howling outside started again, this time close by. Stefan went over and looked out. Both the snow and the wind were picking up.

"Maybe we'd better tie up Boris again," Raine said. "I don't think it's a good idea for him to go out looking for other wolves. Phoebe didn't stand a chance with them. It's a good thing you saved her, Cecil."

"One must look out for one's wolves," Cecil said, "though that's something I never imagined I would say."

Stefan shifted around, trying to get comfortable. "How did Jeremy get the stunt mattresses inflated?" he asked. They weren't very full and he could still feel the cold through them. It would be nice to inflate them more.

"They're called air bags now," Raine said.

"Whatever. You said they had to be hooked up to fans to inflate. Where did he find some electricity?"

Cecil coughed. "I knew Alan is never unprepared, so I sent Jeremy back to the trailer to look for power packs. They are self-contained power sources that give you a small amount of electricity you can access through a plug. One of the many miracles of modern life I never imagined when I was a child. I've seen Alan use them in a pinch. There wasn't enough power to inflate the whole air bag, but since we aren't jumping off cliffs onto them, we didn't need more."

Stefan wished Alan were still here. He had a feeling if they'd had the prop master as a companion, the man would have rigged them some miracle contraption to get away.

Now that they had nothing to do, the cramped space inside the shelter began to get on Stefan's nerves. How much longer would they be stuck there? He felt a desperation and a panic growing in him. "We can't stay here, getting more and more buried in the snow, surrounded by wolves. What if Boris gets free, or the wolves outside decide hunger is more important than fear? We have to get away."

"We can't do anything in the dark," Raine said, "unless we do something dramatic. Jeremy told me about the pyrotechnics he found. Maybe we should set them off. People will be able to see them from a long way away at night. Then they'll know something is wrong."

"No," Cecil said. "Too dangerous. Movie-set pyrotechnics take a trained expert. They aren't like fireworks people set off in their gardens on holidays."

"Cecil's right," Stefan said reluctantly. "Besides, most of those complex movie types would be set off with electronic charges, and we don't have any electricity to do it, unless we find some more power packs." He hated to admit it, but there was nothing they could do until morning. They were stuck, and if the snow continued, he didn't think they could count on a rescue tomorrow either.

"We should try to get some sleep then," Raine said. "This day has gone on forever."

No one said anything for a long time after that, and Stefan thought both Cecil and Raine were asleep, judging by their breathing. He was getting very tired of listening to people breathe, and he was cold, too cold to fall asleep. It was a good thing they were all crammed together and that they had the wolves, because they really would have frozen without them. Boris settled down against his back, and as Stefan lay there, he could feel his muscles relaxing from the heat radiating off the wolf.

Tomorrow, either someone would come to get them or they'd get away by themselves. At least he would get away and go for help. He couldn't stand any more worry about Cecil and Jeremy, and he'd go crazy if he felt too much more snow on him. The thought of it made his skin crawl. If only they had skis, or sleds, or snowboards. If they got down the cliff, they could just take off. Maybe he could find something that would work, for at least himself and Raine. Trying to picture Cecil on skis or a snowboard just didn't work, but they could leave him with Jeremy while they went for help. As soon as they told someone Cecil was ill, people would mount a rescue operation.

His stomach was churning. The one sausage hadn't filled him up. He thought of his house, and how warm the kitchen felt after his mom had been simmering chili on the stove all day. As soon as he got home, she'd make some for him if he asked. And he was sure he could convince her to make some of her brownies too, the ones with the extra chocolate bits. He closed his eyes, thinking how good it would all taste.

Either the cold or the sound of Jeremy's wheezing woke Stefan sometime later. Boris was no longer next to him. Only a few embers remained of the fire and he couldn't feel any heat coming off them. The cold was so sharp it hurt to draw the air into him. He knew it would be agony to drag himself away from the skins to add wood to the fire, but everyone else was too dead asleep to do it for him. If he didn't get up, the fire would go out completely, and the cold would just get worse.

He got up and went to the fire, thankful Raine had the foresight to bring in extra wood. It took him a few moments for his eyes to adjust to the dark and then he saw Boris. The wolf stood by the door, ears alert, the fur on the back of his neck raised. Stefan took a stick from the fire and lifted the flap, waving the glowing tip of it in front of him. Three sets of eyes glowed at him from the darkness, silent and staring.

Stumbling over Boris, Stefan stepped back and dropped the flap. He went to the fire and added all the extra wood. When the fire blazed up, Stefan felt like he could take a breath again, telling himself there was no way the wolves would try to get in with a fire inside. Boris growled and Stefan went over to take his collar. "Easy, boy. You can't go out there." His feet were so cold he tried to lead Boris back to the fire, so he could warm them there, but the wolf wouldn't move. Stefan checked his leash. It was securely fastened, so even if Boris tried to go out, he wouldn't be able to get free.

The rest of him was starting to freeze, and Stefan bundled back under one of the skins, covering his head, trying to fold himself as small as possible, waiting to warm up. He was tired, but sleep wouldn't come. He heard Phoebe whimpering. Was she dreaming of wolves attacking her? Did those wolves nearly starve every winter? He couldn't imagine spending months being cold and hungry, knowing if you didn't move to find food, you would die.

He knew he wouldn't be able to sleep again, not with the knowledge that the wolves were right outside. Jeremy's breathing was getting more and more wheezy, and it was hard not to listen for the boy's next breath, to see if it was better or worse. He was unable to shut the sound out. Cecil's breathing wasn't much better; it was shallow and raspy, like the noise of a distant saw.

Morning came only by a lightening of the gray. The fire was nearly out again, down to embers. Stefan turned on his side, wondering if he had managed to doze a little. The movement made him want to cry out in pain. Every part of him ached no matter which way he moved. He got to his feet slowly, praying the wolves weren't still waiting outside the door. Even if the wolves weren't in sight, he didn't like the thought of going out to try to find more wood, knowing an unseen wolf could be watching him. He went to the flap where Boris still lay. The wolf's ears were alert, but he appeared more relaxed than he had in the night. Stefan lifted the edge and looked out. He didn't see anything but snow on the ground and more snow falling.

Raine came up beside him, yawning. "When is it ever going to stop?"

"This might be one of those storms of the century people talk about," Stefan said, trying not to think too much about the snow, but he couldn't stop thinking about the cold, so sharp now it was like a knife's edge against his skin.

"We have to get more wood," Raine said.

"The wolves were right outside during the night. I don't see them now, but we'll have to be careful."

They went out of the shelter and immediately spotted the wild wolves up the hill by the kitchen area, digging in the snow. The white-eyed wolf lifted his head to watch Stefan and Raine.

"They must still smell food there," Raine said. "I don't think we can get rid of them. What can we use to scare them off?"

"Maybe we don't need to," Stefan said as the

three wolves stopped foraging and took off into the trees. "I wonder if they are more scared of us in the daytime. Does that make sense?"

"I don't know. I'm just glad they're gone."

"We have to do something, now, this morning," Stefan said, brushing at the snow on his face. "They aren't going to stay gone. I'm not sitting around waiting for someone to rescue us. Do you know how to snowboard?"

"Sure, snowboard and ski. We go every year right after the Sun Valley film festival. Well, I snowboard and my mother goes to a spa. You didn't find any snowboards, did you?"

"No, but I have an idea, a couple of ideas actually." He didn't want to tell her in case neither of them worked. "I'm going to go look at a few things to see what's possible. I'll be back in a minute."

He went to the skimmers first, examining how the tube weapons were held on. The skimmer itself was made of some lightweight material, and when Stefan unhooked the bungee cords that held it to the trailer, he could lift up the front of it without too much effort. His skimmer-as-sled idea might work, but it was chancier than his other.

The next step was to see if they had enough of

the big extension cords to climb down from the top of the cliff to the bottom. If they tied them together and knotted them at intervals, he and Raine would have handholds down. Then all he'd need was more gaffer tape and the cooler lids. With those two items he was pretty sure he could fashion makeshift snowboards. If they were going to go for help, it would be a lot faster to snowboard than to walk, even if he wasn't that great at it.

Excited that he had a plan to carry out, Stefan went back to the shelter to find their wolves and Kep sitting in a row outside the door, sweaters wrapped around their heads and ears and tied on top in big bows. Cords were attached to all their collars, and Jeremy held the ends.

Before he could ask Jeremy what was going on, Cecil shuffled out of the shelter, his eyes bloodshot. When he saw the animals, he said, "Am I missing a canine beauty pageant, perhaps?"

"Whatever it is, it wasn't my idea," Stefan said.

Jeremy pointed up toward the trailers. "Raine thinks she can find some pyrotechnics that aren't dangerous. There is a kind that just makes loud noises. She said if she found some she could scare off the other wolves to get some more firewood, but she wanted me to cover our guys' ears so they don't get scared too."

"She's in the prop trailer? She didn't take Cecil's lighter, did she?" Jeremy still wore faint traces of the paint that had spilled in there. A lighter could be disaster.

Cecil held it up. "No, I told her last night it's almost out of fluid."

Stefan's relief lasted only seconds.

"She made a torch instead," Jeremy said. "It was awesome! She took the leg of a chair and wrapped one of the sweaters around it. When she lit it, it really sparked!"

Chapter 19

ESCAPE

"No, no, no! Cecil, keep everybody where they are!" Stefan yelled as he took off to the trailer, forcing himself to run, expecting to see an explosion at any second. When he got to the prop trailer, he climbed up to the opening, screaming Raine's name. At the top he peered down into the opening and saw a wavering glow. "Raine, get out of there!"

"I will," she called. He couldn't see her, but he could tell from the light she was just out of his view. "I found some flares, but I'm still looking for squibs. They're the ones that make the noise."

"Raine, get the torch out of there now! It's dangerous!"

He was about to try to squeeze in to get it himself when the torchlight moved toward the opening and he could see Raine. She lifted it above her head as she climbed up far enough so that her head and shoulders were out in the open. "Don't get all agitated," she said. "I'm being careful."

He grabbed the torch from her hand and plunged the flaming part down into the snow. It sputtered, then went out.

"What did you do that for?" She gathered up some snow like she was going to throw a snowball at him.

"There's paint spilled in there that's probably flammable. If a fire started and spread, the pyrotechnics would go off and you'd be blown to bits. No more Raine. That's why I did it."

"Oh," she said. "I didn't think of that. I was just trying to help. I really, really just want to get out of this place." Stefan was surprised at how down she sounded. It wasn't like her at all, and he tried to think of something to say to make her feel better.

"Don't worry about it," he said. "I need your help on something else. You said you knew how to snowboard; well, here's what we're going to do." He explained his idea and then said, "But we need long cords and more gaffer tape. Can you climb back into the camera trailer for more cords? I can knot some handholds in them while you use the gaffer tape to start making boot holders on the cooler lids. When we get to the bottom of the cliff, we're going to have to tape our boots all the way on, but it will go a lot quicker if there are already some tape pockets in the right spots to begin with."

"I can do that," she said, more enthused again. "I don't know how well it's going to work, but I'm willing to give it a try. Cooler lids! And no stunt people to do it for me! This is great!" She took off toward the camera trailer and then stopped. "Wait, what's your lead foot? If I'm going to make snowboards, I want to get that part right."

"I lead with my left," Stefan said, heading back to the shelter. While Raine was back in the camera trailer, he'd have to figure out how to tell Jeremy and Cecil about the plan. He hoped that after the last time they'd left the two of them alone, Jeremy would be cautious enough just to stay put in the shelter.

Only Jeremy was outside the shelter when Stefan reached it, busy untying the sweaters from the wolves' heads. Kep still had his on, but he was trying to shake it off. "I saw Raine get out the trailer without anything, so I guessed the fireworks idea is off, right? Couldn't she find any?"

"No. Listen, Jeremy. We have a plan. Where's Cecil?"

"He went inside to lie down. He said he was really, really tired." Boris, restless, circled around Jeremy, winding his leash around the boy's legs. "Here, can you hold the leashes and untangle him?" Jeremy asked, holding the ends out to Stefan. "It's hard to untie the sweaters and hold on at the same time." Boris took that moment to give a hard pull, which jerked Jeremy's legs out from under him. The boy fell to the ground and the wolf pulled harder. The knot holding the cord to the collar came undone. The wolf immediately ran off in the direction of the kitchen area. Phoebe strained at her own leash and Stefan didn't act quickly enough to grab it. Jeremy lost hid hold and she ran off after Boris, the leash dragging behind. Kep barked and tried to follow, but Stefan managed to catch the little dog. "Come back!" Jeremy yelled, trying to get up.

Stefan scanned the surroundings but didn't see the wild wolves. "Let those two go for right now.

I want to tell you and Cecil about the plan." He held out a hand to help Jeremy up. "Kep, you'll just have to stick with us."

They went inside and Stefan thought Cecil had gone back to sleep.

"Come back outside," he whispered to Jeremy. After Stefan explained the plan, Jeremy asked, "How long do you think it will take?" Stefan could tell the boy was scared at being left, so he tried to sound reassuring. "It shouldn't take long at all. It's all downhill. We'll be back with help before you know it." He wasn't going to tell Jeremy or Raine the weak link in his idea. Even once people knew they were in trouble, there was still the problem of rescuers getting back to the lodge. He just hoped that because the wind had died down, a helicopter could make it up to Cecil.

Jeremy still looked scared, so Stefan said, "Why don't you finish getting the sweater off Kep and take him inside so he'll stay warm." The little dog had given up trying to get his sweater bow off himself and lay in the snow with a resigned look on his face. He perked up when Jeremy picked him up and licked at the boy's face as Jeremy carried him inside.

Phoebe and Boris were still up by the kitchen

area, sniffing the ground and the debris, like they were examining every inch the wild wolves had walked on. Phoebe found a bone and settled down to chew on it. Stefan debated with himself about whether he should go get the wolves and put them back on leashes. If the white-eyed wolf came back, he didn't know what their wolves would do, but he also knew Phoebe and Boris were hungry. If he tried to pull them away from where they smelled food, they might decide to snap at him. Dogs could give a person a nasty bite if you tried to take their food away from them, so it made sense wolves might do the same.

He headed back to the cliff edge instead. They'd just left Jeremy's harness where he'd taken it off, and it was already under a few inches of snow. Stefan kicked the snow off it and picked it up, untangling the end of the cord from the tree branch and trunk. He didn't want it getting in the way when they needed to tie on the climbing rope.

Raine brought him enough cables and cords to climb down a much taller cliff than the one they stood on. At least they had one supply in abundance. His rumbling stomach reminded him of what they didn't have.

"I'm going to work on the snowboards," she said, "and get Jeremy to collect some wood so they'll stay warm while we're gone."

Intent on knotting the cords, Stefan lost track of time. When he was done he had a climbing rope knotted about every foot. He tied one end around the tree, satisfied the plan would work. As soon as Raine was ready, they could get going. It felt good to know they'd be getting away.

Raine had just brought the snowboards to him and they were examining the boot pockets when Jeremy ran up. "Cecil's really sick again!" he yelled. "Hurry!"

The look on the boy's face was one of pure panic, and Stefan knew it must be bad. The three of them took off for the shelter. Stefan pushed through the flap to find Cecil huddled on the ground clutching his chest and moaning. Stefan felt alarm wash over him. What was he supposed to do? He knelt down and saw that Cecil was having trouble breathing. "Jeremy, find something to put under his head. Cecil, let me help you lie back, you'll breathe better." Raine helped him prop the old man up. Stefan desperately searched his brain for an idea of what to do. He couldn't think of one.

"It's okay, Cecil," Raine said. "It's okay."

They all stayed in place for what seemed like hours, but was probably only a few minutes. Stefan hadn't noticed Kep earlier, but now the little dog came up and joined them, staring at Cecil right along with them. Slowly Cecil's breathing eased, and his face smoothed out like the pain was going away. He closed his eyes and spoke in a voice so soft Stefan had to lean in close to hear. "I'm so sorry, children. I'm afraid my heart is not quite up to this adventure."

"It's okay," Raine said again. "We'll be out of here soon, someplace nice and warm."

Jeremy brought over all the skins and they covered Cecil up. He kept his eyes closed, murmuring something that sounded like "thank you." When it looked like he was comfortable, Stefan pulled Raine and Jeremy outside.

"Change of plans. Jeremy, do you know how to snowboard?" Jeremy shook his head. "Okay," Stefan said. "It doesn't matter. We're *all* getting out of here. Cecil needs a hospital. We can't wait any longer. Even if we can't get across the bridge yet, someone in those houses on this side of the river should be able to call for help, maybe get a helicopter. We're lowering the skimmers down the cliff. Once they're down, I'll be in one with Cecil and Jeremy, you'll have to take the other. Raine can snowboard."

Jeremy and Raine just stared at him.

"Um, Stefan, you know the skimmers don't really work, right?" Raine said. "They're just props. They don't fly. They don't do anything. We can't skim across the snow in them."

"I'm not crazy. I figured out a way to use a skimmer as a sled. We need to hurry, though. The sooner we get Cecil to a hospital, the better it will be for him." That much he remembered from his mom talking about her job.

"Cecil is much bigger than Jeremy. Do you really think we can lower him down?" Raine asked.

"He'd be too heavy to lift up, but all we have to do when we lower him is make sure we don't let the cord slip out of our hands. We'll make him a harness and we'll tie one end to the tree just in case. It will break his fall if something goes wrong."

"That makes sense," Raine said, "if we can make him a harness that holds together."

"What should we do first?" Jeremy asked.

"We see if we can get the skimmer to the edge of the cliff. Come on!"

They raced over to the trailers and unhooked the bungee cords that held the skimmers in place on the trailers. As Stefan had hoped, between the three of them they managed to carry the props over to the edge of the cliff.

"We need the tarps from the shelter too," Stefan said after they had lowered the second skimmer to the ground.

"Jeremy and I will get them. I have to go get something to get Kep down too. I'm not leaving him here." Raine and Jeremy went off in the direction of the shelter, and Stefan hoped whatever she thought up, it wouldn't take too much time to find. They couldn't have Cecil wait for the dog.

Stefan began to make the harness for Cecil, first examining the one he'd made for Jeremy to remember how he'd done it. It didn't take long, and by the time Jeremy was back, he was done and had tied one end around the tree trunk.

With the tarps and the cables, Stefan figured he could make a sling for the first skimmer. With the skimmer resting on the tarp and the cables run through the holes where the bungee cords had been, it would be the quickest way to get the prop down below. Jeremy helped him while

Stefan explained what they were doing. "We're going to send you down first, then Cecil. After that we'll send the skimmers. We'll need you at the bottom to get the tarp off from around them. Cecil can get in one to stay warm while we come down. Okay? If anything goes wrong, you just take off with Cecil."

"I still don't understand how I'm supposed to use the skimmer," Jeremy said. "It doesn't steer."

"It's like a sled without runners, so you're going to steer with the side weapons." Stefan stopped working with the tarps to show Jeremy what he was talking about. He unclamped one of the fasteners on the tube and let the back end of it drop into the snow. "The tube pivots around on this bracket. When you push it down into the snow, it will turn the skimmer in the same direction. If you lift up it up out of the snow and push down on the other one, you'll turn in the other direction. It's like how you use a canoe paddle to turn a canoe. The canoe always wants to turn to the side you're paddling on." At least that was the way the skimmer idea worked in Stefan's head. He didn't know if it would actually work. "All you have to do is zigzag down the hill so you don't pick up too much speed. Do you think you can do that?"

"I think so," Jeremy said, "but I've never been in a canoe."

"That's okay. It's easy." It wasn't really, without a little practice, but there wasn't time for a lesson.

Raine came back as they were about to lift one of the skimmers onto the tarp.

"Did you find what you need?" Stefan asked.

One of the costume sweaters was around her neck and she grabbed hold of a sleeve of it. "I'm going to tie Kep up in this and then tie it around my neck like a baby carrier."

"Okay," Stefan said. Better her than him.

Lowering Jeremy was much easier than it had been to bring him up. It only seemed to take a few minutes.

"It feels like he's at the bottom," Raine said. "I don't feel any more weight on the rope."

"Go look and I'll keep hold," Stefan said.

Jeremy shouted something but Stefan couldn't understand.

"He's clear and he wants you to lift the cable back up."

Stefan hauled the harness back up as fast as he could. "Let's go get Cecil," he said, hoping the man would be strong enough to walk. When they got back to the shelter it was clear Cecil was too weak. He could barely lift his head.

"Let's just push him on the air bags," Raine suggested. "The ground is sloped down enough to get him to the edge of the cliff, and if we're walking beside it holding on, it won't go too fast."

They both tried to explain what they were doing, but Cecil either didn't understand or didn't care. He just kept closing his eyes. Stefan took apart a section of the shelter so they could just push the mattress right out. Kep jumped on and lay down next to Cecil like it was the most normal thing in the world to be riding around on an air mattress. Phoebe joined them, watching Kep but making no move to get on herself. The mattress slid easily over the snow, and the movement or being out in the cold air roused Cecil some. He looked more alert and, once they were next to the cliff, even had enough strength to sit up so they could help him into the harness once they were next to the cliff.

Stefan still couldn't get him to say anything. It was as if the old man was listening to someone or something inside him, too occupied to pay attention to much of the outside world. Once he was in the harness, Raine wrapped a skin around him and tied it.

"It will help protect him from scraping against the rocks," she said, "and help keep him warm at the bottom."

It was harder to keep a grip when they lowered Cecil, and Stefan felt the pain in his rib as he tried to keep the rope feeding out at a slow pace. He held his breath until he felt the tension on the cord rope disappear. "He's at the bottom!" Raine said. "I'll tell you when he's clear. I hope Jeremy can help him out. Cecil's trying to stand up, but he's having trouble. He's leaning on Jeremy. Oh no!"

"What happened?"

"They both fell, but Jeremy is helping him. Now they're just sitting. Oh good, Jeremy is rewrapping the skin around him. It had come lose. Bring the harness up!"

When the harness was back at the top, Raine asked, "What about the wolves?"

Boris had joined them too, and both wolves were watching them expectantly, as if all their activity might result in the appearance of food.

"I don't think the wolves are going to let us fasten harnesses on them and lower them down," Stefan said. "We're going to have to leave them here and try to get help as fast as we can." He couldn't see any other choice except to leave them behind.

"Let's get the skimmer down, so Cecil can get in it." They followed the same plan as they had with Cecil, throwing the end of the cable over the branch of the tree to help them lower the prop. It went down easily for the first few feet, but then they heard it bump against the face of the cliff. There was a distinct cracking sound as it hit.

"I don't think it's going to hold together," Raine said. "The cliff is too jagged, and we can't swing it out far enough away to stay clear."

"I know, let's just keep going though. Maybe it won't be in too bad of shape once we get it to the bottom."

They let out another few feet and then Jeremy yelled something. All of a sudden there was no more weight on the rope. When they looked over, they could see why. The skimmer had slid right out of one end of the tarp and fallen to the ground, splitting into pieces, like a broken egg.

"Great," Raine said. "We'll have to try the other skimmer and hope it doesn't fall or hit too hard. We can run more cables around it."

Stefan hauled the tarp back up. "No, it will take too long. I have a better idea. We need to get the other stunt mattress."

"I'm not using an air bag to sled down the lower part of the mountain. It was fine to use one to slide Cecil over with us holding onto it and walking alongside. But there's no way to steer sitting on it. Even though the lower part of the mountain isn't as steep as a ski slope, it's a lot steeper than the parking lot." Raine looked at him as if he had gone crazy.

"We're not using the mattresses as sleds. We're going to use them to do a skimmer drop, just like an egg drop in school."

"You've really lost me. None of my tutors ever did an egg drop."

"I'll explain while we get the other one." She hesitated but then followed him as he jogged toward the shelter, Stefan talking as fast as he could. "Everybody does it in science class. You get an egg, a raw one, and you have to figure out the best way to protect it when you drop it from a high place. The ones with air insulating them are always the ones that make it. The others usually just end up a broken mess."

"I still don't get it."

"We're wrapping the skimmer up in the stunt mattresses to protect it. We'll tie it to the end of the rope instead of the tarp, and then when it goes over the cliff, it won't break if it falls or bumps on a rock. Just like a giant egg drop. Wait, we need something else." He detoured back to the skimmer trailers, picking up the discarded bungee cords. "We'll use these to fasten the mattresses around it."

Raine shook her head like she didn't believe him, but she didn't argue; so as long as she kept going along with the plan, it didn't matter.

They dragged the mattress across the snow to the cliff edge and lifted the skimmer on it. When they laid the other mattress on top of the skimmer, Raine said, "Skimmer sandwich."

"I'd rather have a real sandwich," he muttered, handing Raine one end of the bungee cord. "I think this is going to work. We just have to get it fastened to the end of the cord rope."

"Uh-oh," Raine said. "There's smoke coming from the prop trailer."

Chapter 20

HUNTED

As *Stefan turned to* look, a tremendous boom sounded and the prop trailer exploded, sending bits of metal and flaming debris into the air.

The boom echoed back from the cliffs. This time when the rumbling started up the mountain, he knew what it was.

"Is that what I think it is?" Raine whispered. They looked at each other in horror.

"Help me push the skimmer over!" Stefan yelled.

"But it's not attached to the rope!"

"We don't have time. Just help me push!"

It took only seconds to slide the skimmer off the cliff. It sailed out and then down, but Stefan didn't wait to see it land. The rumbling had turned to a roar.

"Go, go, go!" he yelled. "Get down the rope! I'll be right behind you."

"Where's Kep?" Raine screamed.

Stefan looked behind him and saw the little dog crouched on one side of the tree. "Go!" he yelled. "I've got him!" Picking up the dog, he unzipped his coat far enough to put the animal down inside against his chest and then zipped it up again, hoping Kep wouldn't squirm too much and fall out.

When Raine saw what he was doing she grabbed the cord and started to slide down. "Stefan, we forgot the cooler lids and the tape!"

Stefan reached behind him and flung everything he could pick up over the edge. Grabbing hold of the rope, he let himself go over the edge, looking back toward the remains of the lodge to see a colossal mass of snow hurtling toward him. He watched, paralyzed, and then he felt Kep struggling to get out of his coat. He forced himself to slide as he fast as he could, trying at the same time to see how far Raine was below him, not wanting to slam into her. He was amazed to see Boris and Phoebe making their way down the cliff next to him like mountain goats, leaping from one ledge to the next and sliding where there were no ledges.

The avalanche surged over the side of the cliff, smashing into the tree that held the rope. The tree tipped like it was being uprooted, and Stefan dropped down, nearly losing his grip as the snow from above pelted him. He saw Raine at the bottom, wading through the snow toward Cecil and Jeremy. Then the tree gave way and Stefan fell the last few feet, the pain in his ribs slicing through him.

He must have passed out because when he opened his eyes, Raine's face was above his and he could feel her trying to pull him to his feet.

"Stefan, wake up! Are you hurt?"

There was no real reason to answer, because he thought he'd forgotten what it felt like not to hurt. He struggled to his feet, trying to brush the snow off. Boris came up and pushed his nose into Stefan's hand.

"Hi boy," Stefan said, too weary to pet the animal. The wolf didn't look any worse for wear from his trip down the cliff. He realized he didn't see or feel Kep in his jacket, but then he spotted the dog over next to Cecil and Phoebe.

"That was very scary." Raine's face was pale. "I'm really sorry I was so stupid about the pyrotechnics. You had me worried there for a minute. You were out cold."

"Cold is a good word for it," Stefan said. "Why didn't the avalanche bury me?"

"You were lucky; the main part of it missed you. You were even luckier the tree missed you." She pointed at the evergreen, the remains of it sunk in the snow nearby. "Do you think you can move? Jeremy already has the mattresses off the skimmer, but we're going to need your help to get Cecil in," Raine said. "Jeremy told me you already explained to him how it was going to work."

Stefan tried and failed to force himself to move. Maybe he'd just stay there and send everyone else off for help. He could just lie back in the snow and close his eyes.

"Stefan, are you sure you are okay?" Raine took hold of his jacket. "We really need to get Cecil out of here."

When he looked over at the old man, the sight of the pain on Cecil's pale face shocked him back into what had to be done.

"We need to open this up," Stefan moved over to the skimmer and unhooked the latch, pulling it back. "We'll get Cecil in first."

"We need to put Kep in too," Raine said. "There's no way he can follow us in all this snow."

"We can put him on Cecil's lap," Jeremy said. He went over to the mattress where Kep lay and picked up the dog.

Stefan hoped the plan wasn't too crazy. The skimmer might be too heavy with both Cecil and Jeremy inside. It might not slide on the surface of the snow at all.

They helped Cecil in, practically lifting him up over the edge. Jeremy put Kep inside and then climbed in himself. Kep licked Cecil's face and the man opened his eyes. Stefan was glad to see there was no confusion in Cecil's eyes, only pain.

"If all the world's a stage, why don't we have an audience for this little adventure?" Cecil asked.

"You will, Cecil," Raine said. "Think of all the interviews you are going to do. After this, everyone will be clamoring for your story. It will make a great chapter in your memoirs."

The old man closed his eyes again and laid his head back.

"They need to get going," Stefan said. "Jeremy, don't let yourself pick up very much speed. The more you turn back and forth, the slower you will go, and the better control you'll have. We're going to give you a push. Are you sure you understand how to steer?"

"I think," Jeremy said, "so I want to try it." Only a gentle shove was necessary. Jeremy was off down the hill going really, really fast. Phoebe chased after the skimmer, barking.

"Steer!" Stefan yelled. "Turn! Slow down!"

Jeremy pushed down on one of the tube weapons, sending up a plume of snow. The vehicle turned just like it was supposed to. Now Stefan was glad there was so much snow. The skimmer would have gotten out of control on a slope without much powder. He watched until he saw Jeremy make the next turn. Even if he and Raine couldn't manage to snowboard, Jeremy would at least be able to find someone to help Cecil.

"That means we should go too," Raine said, picking up the cooler lids. "Let me tape your feet on." Raine had already figured out which way to wrap, and within a minute Stefan was fastened on. He tried to stand and immediately fell down.

"They aren't the greatest but I think they're going to work," Raine said, finishing hers. She got to her feet and slid a few yards down the hill, twisting around to look back up at Stefan.

Stefan got back up and slid a few more feet, trying to get a feel for how to balance. He fell down again. This had been a stupid idea.

"I'm going ahead," Raine said. "Jeremy's stopped partway down. I don't know if he's waiting for us or there's a problem, so I'm going to catch up with them. Are you okay?"

"Fine," Stefan said, irritated at himself. "Tell him not to wait for us." Raine took off, and even though she wobbled a bit at the start, she picked up a smooth motion, trailing after the skimmer effortlessly. She hadn't been exaggerating when she said she knew how to snowboard.

Stefan tried again and managed to travel a little ways before he fell. He got back up. Boris loped beside him, sticking close, either because the wolf realized he was hopeless at cooler-lid boarding or the wolf was just too worn out to dash around like he normally did.

It wasn't impossible to make the lid do what he wanted, but Stefan fell several more times. He was concentrating so hard on his balance he had no warning. One minute it was just him and Boris and the sound of the lid on the snow. Then a snarling mass of gray fur came out of nowhere, lunging at Boris, knocking him into

Stefan. Stefan lost his balance and fell, sliding down the hill. Boris rolled and then leaped to his feet. Both wolves flew at each other, twisting and biting, savage noises coming from their throats. The white-eyed wolf tried to get at Boris's neck, but Boris turned just in time, and the wolf caught him on the shoulder instead. The fangs sank in and Boris gave a howl of pain.

Stefan pushed off his boots, got to his feet and picked up the lid, putting it in front of him like a shield. He screamed at the white-eyed wolf, trying to distract it.

Another wolf, a black one, exploded from the trees and leaped at the white-eyed wolf, shoving it away from Boris, biting and snapping at it in a frenzy. It was Natasha. Stefan had never imagined such fury in an animal, and he didn't know how the white-eyed wolf could continue to fight for long. Suddenly the white-eyed wolf dropped to the ground and Natasha leaped at it. When she was almost on it, the white-eyed wolf vaulted upward, catching her by the throat.

She gave one high-pitched yelp and then fell to the ground, unmoving, the blood pouring from a gaping wound in her neck. The white-eyed wolf, its sides heaving, turned back to Boris, who was struggling to get up. Stefan ran forward, putting himself between the two wolves. They circled each other, Stefan holding the shield in front of him, never letting the wolf get a clear shot at Boris. His bootless feet were freezing and he knew he couldn't keep moving forever. He just had to hope the wolf would give up. It took a step closer and Stefan fell back, nearly stepping on Boris.

He heard weird screeches and whooping noises, and when he turned his head enough to see, he couldn't believe it. Jeremy and Raine were running toward him, lit flares held high in their hands, yelling what sounded like war cries.

The white-eyed wolf snapped once in their direction, and then he turned and bolted off into the trees. Boris limped over to Natasha and lay down beside her, licking her face. Natasha's eyes were wide open, staring into nothing. Stefan knew she was dead.

He sank down into the snow, closed his own eyes and then opened them again. He thought he heard more rumbling. If it was another avalanche, he knew he couldn't go any farther. Raine yelled and pointed down the hill. Down the mountain, in the distance, a fleet of snowmobiles roared toward them.

Raine and Jeremy jumped up and down waving their flares as Stefan watched, too exhausted to move. His first thought was to wonder where they'd gotten the flares, and then he remembered Raine saying she'd found some in the prop trailer. He hadn't realized she'd taken some with her.

The snowmobiles reached the skimmer first and encircled it. Some of the people on them got off and hurried to the open canopy. Stefan could see Cecil raising one arm and he felt relieved the man was still conscious. That had to be a good sign. Cecil waved his hand in their direction and soon some of the snowmobiles were moving again. Stefan thought he spotted someone with pink hair, but he couldn't tell if it was just a person in a pink hat or if it was really Heather.

Hans was on one of the first ones to reach them, riding behind a man in some sort of official-looking snow gear. As soon as the snowmobile came to a halt, the wolf trainer leaped from it and stumbled to where Natasha lay, falling to the ground and burying his face in her fur. Boris nudged in next to him and the man put one arm around the wolf, drawing him in close.

Mark was right behind Hans. He swept Raine and Jeremy up in a giant hug, all of them talking at the same time. Within seconds there were people everywhere, most of them unfamiliar to Stefan and speaking something other than English.

Stefan closed his eyes again but opened them when he heard Heather's voice. "Stefan, are you okay?" He opened his eyes to see his aunt reaching for him like she was going to try to hug him. "Your mom is going to have a cow when she hears about this, right after she kills me for leaving you alone. Tell me you're okay."

"Heather, I'm good," he said, holding up his hand to stave her off. "I've just got a rib that isn't so good, so let's save the hugs, okay? Wow, am I glad to see you. How'd you find out we were in trouble?"

Mark appeared next to her before she could answer, Raine and Jeremy on either side of him. "That's quite a tale," the director said. "The cook had her husband bring her into the village because she cut herself and needed stitches on her hand. We heard a very strange tale about hungry wolves roaming the lodge. One of them came into the kitchen while she was prepping food for breakfast and frightened her so much she cut her arm with a knife."

"I knew it was blood!" Raine said, a big smile

on her face. "You wouldn't believe what we really thought happened to the cook."

"I want to hear everything that happened," Mark said, "but first you all need to be checked out by a doctor."

"That's a good plan," Stefan got slowly to his feet. "And afterward, I'd like to sit in front of a roaring fire. Can that happen? Raine could even build it for me. She's pretty good with fire, except we should make sure the furniture is bolted to the floor."

Raine made a motion like she was going to throw snow at him, and Stefan didn't bother to duck, thinking a little snow wouldn't hurt him now.

EPILOGUE

LONDON, TWO WEEKS LATER

Stefan pretended to blast at imaginary creatures outside the viewport while he waited for filming to start. He couldn't believe the intricate detail on the interior sets of the spaceship. It was as if he were really on an actual spacecraft, with the lights and the control panels and people wandering around in costumes. Even the guy standing nearby eating a yogurt parfait couldn't spoil it for him.

When he swung around in his chair to reach for a screen farther away, the pain in his side reminded him to take it a little easier. His cracked rib had turned out to be three cracked ribs, plus pneumonia and mild frostbite. After the snowmobile rescue, he'd spent a few days in the hospital, then ended up in a hotel in Prague, under orders from the doctors and Mark to stay put in his and Heather's suite, order room service, and watch movies until he felt better. Stefan didn't argue. Besides Amanda popping in every day with schoolwork, it had been like a luxury vacation. He'd even worked on some new imitations, including a great one of the little alien in an old movie called *E.T.* When he had the chance, he'd show Mark, and maybe even Cecil and Jeremy.

Filming had shut down for two weeks while the studio had considered what to do. Stefan had a few bad days when Jeremy reported a rumor that the movie would be canceled because it would have to go over budget to finish, but that was a short-lived fear. The media found out about their adventure and suddenly everyone was clamoring to see the movie behind the disaster.

Boris and Phoebe were reported to be recovering nicely, and it turned out Inky was fine too. The wolves were almost getting more press than the humans, and Natasha was hailed as the heroine of it all, giving up her life to save Boris. Stefan hadn't seen Hans, but he imagined the wolf trainer would mourn her for a long time.

When the paparazzi found out Raine was in Paris, where her mother had taken her to recuperate, she was mobbed. He saw images of her on television news with security guards guiding her through crowds of photographers. Much had been made of Cecil, how he had survived a heart attack and was still determined to finish the movie. Stefan had seen him once in Prague and thought he looked too frail to keep working, but Cecil had assured him Mark was adjusting the script to make his scenes a bit easier.

Stefan was just ready to get on with it. Filming had been scheduled to start the day before, but Raine's mother had demanded more money for her to finish the movie. There was a lot of grumbling going on about it, according to Heather. He could tell it was adding to the tension on set. Everybody but Mark seemed edgy, and Heather had said it was because some movie people were so superstitious, they were convinced the film was now cursed.

That had made Stefan laugh, but Heather claimed it was a really bad atmosphere for a set, according to her new boyfriend, one of the grips who worked with the lights.

Now that everyone knew he had been part of the adventure too, Stefan hoped it meant he was safe from being fired. Sherman the producer hadn't said anything to him beyond asking if he was well enough to work, but Jeremy had passed along a rumor that the actor Raine wanted, Justin Seton, was now very interested in the film. There was no way Stefan was going to give anyone a reason to replace him. He knew he could do the work, especially as long as Raine hadn't gone back to her movie-star self. If she went back to giving him a death glare every time he made a mistake, he'd get nervous and just make more.

"Stefan, I need to go over the schedule with you and Jeremy," Amanda said, sitting down next to him, Jeremy in tow. Jeremy had been bouncing all over the set with excitement the last half hour, and Stefan wondered how Amanda had managed to capture him.

"Jeremy, please listen," Amanda said. "You and Stefan and Raine have an interview this afternoon with an American television news show. I'll make sure they stay on schedule so you children can get your schoolwork in. I'm told Raine will have her publicist there, and you're to only answer the questions directly asked to you. Raine will answer the rest. Okay?"

"Sure," Stefan said, relieved he wouldn't have to talk much.

"Good. Now I have to check on the schoolroom and make sure it's set up correctly. Jeremy, why don't you stay with Stefan and keep out of everyone's way?"

Stefan motioned to the seat next to him as Amanda walked away. "Jeremy, take a look at this control panel. It's incredible."

Jeremy sat down. "Can I push the buttons?"

"Why not? We can't really blast anything. Let's practice the scene where we're the only ones around who know how to operate the spaceship. I fly and you're in charge of the weapons."

There was clapping behind them and Stefan turned to see Mark and Cecil arriving. More and more people stood up and joined in, and Stefan realized they were all clapping for Cecil's return.

The elderly actor gave a dramatic bow. "No, no, you shouldn't," the man said. Stefan knew Cecil was secretly pleased with the attention.

Before the applause had completely died away, Raine swept in, followed by a small entourage of people, including someone he didn't recognize carrying Kep. He was happy to see the dog wasn't wearing any sweaters, hats, or booties.

Mark went up to her and gave her a hug. He turned to the crowd. "I was going to make a short welcoming speech but I think we'll have more fun if we just get right into filming. We've got a light day scheduled so we can ease back into things." Mark looked so gleeful at the idea of filming, Stefan relaxed a little. Knowing he wouldn't have to attempt a big scene helped a lot.

"Okay," Mark said. "We're doing the scene where Stefan, Raine, Jeremy, and Cecil are in your private quarters on the spaceship, debating whether or not you can trust all the troops on board. The wolves are part of the scene, but they don't have to do anything except lie around and look like family pets. We won't bring them out until we're ready to film. Let's get into place and we'll talk about the reactions I'm looking for."

Stefan walked over to the set that looked like a futuristic living room, with soft gray furniture arranged around a central table that glowed with a map of an imaginary galaxy. Mark showed everyone where they were to sit and immediately began to go over what he wanted. Stefan stayed quiet, figuring they would all have time to talk on the lunch break. Raine hadn't even looked at him.

Mark had only said a few sentences when Raine leaped up, screaming, "I see blood, it's spattered everywhere." She pointed at the table. There was a collective gasp from most of the crew members, though Stefan wasn't sure he could see any blood.

Jeremy got up and nearly fell over one of the chairs, "Where?"

"Cecil!" Raine yelled, pointing at him. "You have blood on you!" She backed away from him like he was going to attack her. "What's happening here?"

Cecil ducked his head for a long moment while everyone waited for him to speak. He raised his head, his eyes bulging out, his face contorted in his swamp-creature features. He gave an evil laugh. "Wouldn't you like to know," he screeched and advanced toward Raine, who was looking horrified. It was so unexpected nobody moved until the old man was within reach of her. He stopped and the two of them grinned, then began laughing so hard Cecil had to sit down.

"Fooled you!" Raine said. "Cecil, that was fabulous! See everyone, we can't have a cursed set because we're going to have too much fun making this movie." She came over to where Stefan and Jeremy stood. "You really believed I saw blood, didn't you?" she asked, smiling.

"I believed it," Stefan said. "Good one." He had to convince Cecil to work with him on that swamp-creature imitation.

"Okay, let's make a movie!" Mark called. "We have battles to fight, creatures to vanquish, and a planet to tame!"